Go ahead and

No one can h.... you. You're no longer in the safe world you know.

You've taken a terrifying step . . .

into the darkest corners of your imagination.

You've opened the door to . . .

the NIGHTMARE room

Read all the books in

the NIGHTMARE room

series by R.L. Stine

the NiGHTMARE rOOm

THRILLOGY 1

Fear Games

R.L. STINE

PARACHUTE PRESS

Collins

An imprint of HarperCollinsPublishers

Fear Games

Copyright © 2001 by Parachute Publishing, L.L.C.

Special thanks to Mr. George Sheanshang

First published in the USA by Avon 2001
First published in Great Britain by Collins 2001
Collins is an imprint of HarperCollins*Publishers* Ltd,
77-85 Fulham Palace Road, Hammersmith, London, W6 8JB

The HarperCollins website address is www.fireandwater.com

1 3 5 7 9 8 6 4 2

ISBN 0 00 712376 0

The author asserts the moral right to be identified
as the author of the work

Printed and bound in Great Britain by
Omnia Books Limited, Glasgow

Welcome . . .

Hello, I'm R.L. Stine. Welcome to a very special *Nightmare Room* book.

It's about a girl named April Powers who joins eleven other kids on a tropical island. The kids are there to play survival games—for a prize of $100,000. But they soon discover that someone else is on the island, someone who doesn't *want* them to survive!

When I started to write this story I realized that it was too big and too frightening to tell in one book. April's story had to be told in *three* books instead of one.

And so the THRILLOGY was born.

Welcome to my *special* nightmare. . . .

the NiGHTMARE room

Fear Games

Part One
This Winter

"I can do magic," April Powers said. "Evil magic."

Her friend Andy Butler snickered. "Cool," he said. "Make me disappear. I don't want to take the algebra test this afternoon."

April didn't smile. "I'm not wasting my magical powers on you. I'm saving them. For Pam."

Andy swept a hand over his short, dark hair. "Pam? What did Pam do this time?"

"What *didn't* she do," April muttered. "She's always on my case. She thinks she's Miss Perfect."

"Pam *is* perfect!" Andy teased.

"She's a perfect idiot," April said, scowling.

They were standing outside the door to the lunchroom. Down the hall, two teachers perched on ladders. They were struggling to hang a purple and gold banner across the hall: GO, APPLEGATE RED DEER!

In the crowded lunchroom, trays clattered, chairs scraped, voices rang off the yellow tile walls. And the slightly sour aroma of fish sticks and macaroni and cheese floated into the hall.

April tugged at the long red plastic earring that always dangled from her left ear. Then she shook her head to straighten her dark bangs. She kept her eyes on the stairs, searching for Pam Largent.

"Do you believe it?" she asked Andy. "Pam told Ricky Jason that I like him and want to go to the valentine's dance with him. Isn't that gross?"

"But you *do* like Ricky," Andy insisted.

April rolled her brown eyes. "You don't get it. It was just her way of making me look like a jerk. Everyone knows that Ricky likes Pam. Pam said it only to make Ricky laugh."

"You're right. I don't get it," Andy said. He flashed a thumbs-up to two guys who pushed past them into the lunchroom. "Hey—save me a seat!"

"Pam *loves* to make me look bad," April continued, watching the stairs. "She has to compete in everything. And she always has to win. When I decided to do my term paper on magic spells through history, guess what topic Pam picked?"

"I give up," Andy said.

April groaned. "Magic spells through history," she said. "Just so she can do it better than me."

She tugged at her earring. She always did it when she was tense or angry. "I'm not a violent person. You know that. Actually, I *hate* violence. But I'd like to rip Pam's face off and hang it from that banner up there!"

Andy laughed. "You're sick."

"I don't think that's sick," April said. "I think it's

only fair. But don't worry. I'm not going to get violent. I'm going to use magic instead."

"If you can't stand her, why do you spend so much time with Pam?" Andy asked.

"You know. Because our parents are all such good friends. I don't have a choice. Every time I turn around—HEY!" She saw the blond ponytail bouncing behind Pam's head as Pam appeared on the stairs.

April gave Andy a shove. "Beat it, okay? Get lost. Time for me to do my nasty little spell."

"Can't I watch?" Andy asked.

April didn't answer. She hurried down the hall to meet Pam.

Pam was the tallest girl at Applegate Middle School. She complained about it: "I'm a freak! The boys are all scared of me!"

But April knew that Pam liked being the tallest, the prettiest, the blondest, the smartest, the funniest . . . and on and on.

"Were you waiting for me?" Pam asked. Her normally creamy white cheeks were pink. Beads of sweat glistened on her forehead.

She had gym just before lunch on Mondays.

April couldn't keep a grin from spreading across her face. "I want to show you something."

"I'm starving!" Pam declared, striding past April to the lunchroom door. "What kind of salad do they have today?"

"No, wait." April hurried to block her path. "It

won't take long. I—I learned some magic."

Pam stopped. Her blue eyes studied April. She laughed. "You want to show me card tricks now? Isn't that a little babyish?"

"I learned some spells," April said. "I was doing research for my term paper. I found a dusty old book in the stacks at the library. I learned how to do some totally amazing things. I—I have powers, Pam. I'm not kidding."

Pam pressed her hand against April's forehead. "You're running a temperature, right? Should I take you to the nurse?"

She hates this, April thought. She hates the idea that I can do something she can't. This is perfect!

April dragged Pam into the lunchroom. She could see Andy watching from a table against the wall.

"Do you pull a bunny from a hat, or what?" Pam asked impatiently. "I am *so* not into magic tricks."

"It's not tricks," April replied. "I told you, I learned spells. And these spells are going to get me an A on my term paper."

"Why are you so hung up about grades?" Pam asked.

"Just watch." April tugged Pam closer to the lunch line. "Let's pick someone, okay? Someone I can cast a spell on."

Both girls gazed around the crowded room.

"How about Merrilee Crane over there?" April said. She pointed to the short, chubby girl with curly red hair who had just carried her lunch tray to the woman at the cash register.

Pam sighed and rolled her eyes. "Okay, fine. Merrilee. Just do it fast, okay?"

Merrilee paid for her lunch, then started across the room with her tray.

"Keep your eye on her," April said in a whisper. She began to mutter strange words to herself. *"Amanoo . . . keela . . ."*

April waved her hands again. *"Kornoo . . . apaka . . . namoo,"* she whispered.

Several kids let out cries as the lunch tray spun from Merrilee's hands. The tray flew up into the air—and came crashing down on the floor. The plates clattered loudly and food spilled around Merrilee's feet.

Merrilee's mouth dropped open in shock. She raised her hands in the air helplessly.

"Hahakoo . . . Bellem . . ." April whispered.

And across the room, Merrilee started to spin. Slowly at first, her arms still above her head. And then faster, spinning awkwardly, stumbling into the spilled food.

"Help me—somebody!" Merrilee screamed. Her face twisted in horror, red hair flying wildly as she spun. "Please—help me!"

She uttered a groan as she slammed hard into the tile wall. Then her body appeared to collapse. And she slumped to the floor and didn't move.

April turned to catch the shocked expression on

Pam's face. Pam had gone pale. Her blue eyes bulged. She was panting rapidly, clenching her hands into tight fists.

"You—you—" Her eyes burned into April's. "How—?"

Pam didn't wait for an answer. "You're a *witch!*" Pam shrieked. Then she whirled away from April and took off, running from the room.

The lunchroom had grown silent. April could hear Pam's thudding footsteps as she ran down the hall.

Against the wall, kids were helping Merrilee to her feet. She kept shaking her head, blinking her eyes, her expression dazed, confused.

Thinking about Pam, April couldn't keep a smile of triumph from spreading across her face.

After school, April started to walk home. A snowstorm that morning had left a powdery dusting of white on the ground. Just enough snow to make the ground slick and shiny. The sky was gray, the sun hidden behind a thick covering of clouds.

"April—wait up!"

April spun around to see Merrilee running across the street, waving both arms. Merrilee's backpack bounced on the shoulders of her blue parka. Her black Skechers kept sliding on the powdery snow.

As Merrilee caught up to April, both girls burst out laughing. They slapped each other high-fives.

"I can't believe it!" Merrilee cried. "I totally can't *believe* it!"

"Pam went for it," April said, her dark eyes glowing gleefully. "We hooked her like a fish on a line!"

Merrilee brushed her coppery hair down with one hand. "You're a genius! A genius! Did Pam really think you were casting a spell on me?"

April nodded, giggling. "She turned purple. I thought she was going to lose her breakfast!"

"But she knows we're friends—right?" Merrilee said. "Didn't she guess that maybe we cooked the whole thing up and rehearsed it?"

April shook her head. "It was too good a performance. I couldn't believe it when you started to spin out of control. How did you do that?"

"I used to take ballet lessons when I was little," Merrilee replied. She sighed. "Unfortunately, I'm not built like a ballet dancer now."

"Well, you're a great twirler," April said. "And I loved it when you stepped into your own food."

"That part was an accident," Merrilee admitted. "I didn't mean to do that. It took me an hour to wash the glop off my shoes!"

They waited for a van filled with teenagers to pass. Then they crossed the street.

"Come to my house and hang out for a while," April said. "I think there's some chocolate cake in the fridge. We can celebrate our great victory over the evil forces of Pam."

Merrilee laughed. "You know what she's doing right now, don't you? She's in the library, searching the shelves for old spell books. She has to top you.

She's going to come to school tomorrow and turn everyone into frogs!"

"Croak-croak," April said. She turned up her driveway and started to search for the house key in her bag. "I'm sure Pam has figured out our little joke by now. She'll be too embarrassed to come to school tomorrow."

Merrilee snickered. "Pam? Embarrassed? You're kidding—right?"

April pulled a stack of mail from the mailbox. Then she opened the front door and led the way into the house. "Take off your wet shoes," she told Merrilee. "You know how crazy Mom is about her wood floors."

April pulled off her coat and backpack and tossed them onto the front stairs. She shuffled through the mail. "Hey—what's this?" She held up a long brown envelope.

Merrilee was brushing her hair in front of the hall mirror. She turned. "You have mail? I never get mail. Never."

April examined the envelope. "It's from something called The Academy. What is that? Ever hear of it?"

Merrilee stepped up beside her friend. "Is it a school?"

"Probably just some company trying to sell phonics workbooks," April said. She started to set the envelope down.

"Open it up!" Merrilee cried. "Let's see what it's about."

April tore open the envelope and pulled out several sheets of heavy white paper. She unfolded them and squinted at the long letter on top. Her eyes scanned the page.

"Weird," she muttered as she started to read. "This is totally weird. . . ."

Dear April Powers:

We have exciting news for you!

The board of directors of The Academy is pleased to inform you that you have been selected from a list of hundreds of honor students.

We wish to invite you to become a member of The Academy at our two-week meeting this spring.

Along with eleven other top students from around the United States, you will be joined by leading figures and celebrities from the fields of government, education, entertainment, sports, and business. A list of these leaders is enclosed.

The meeting will be held on a beautiful, private tropical island in the Caribbean Sea. You and your new friends will have time to use the white sandy beach, explore rock caves, and swim in the warm aqua waters of this tropical paradise.

The island is uninhabited. But comfortable

housing has been built, along with many conveniences.

We have designed your two-week stay as a thrilling, once-in-a-lifetime experience. The Academy begins as a meeting of invited strangers—but ends as a community of friends.

As a new student member of The Academy, you will have a chance to meet and build lasting friendships with the other eleven new student members.

You will also listen to talks by the visiting celebrities and leaders. And you will get to know them all personally at meals and other activities.

And there is more to your Academy stay than making friends and learning from national leaders. You will also be invited to join in a competition we call Life Games.

Life Games are fun, surprising, and very challenging. You have been chosen because you are an achiever. You enjoy the thrill of competing against others.

Once the games get started, you won't want them to end!

You will find the Life Games on our island to be exciting—and very rewarding. The winning student team will divide a prize of $100,000.

We are enclosing a reservation form and pages of questions and answers. Of course, all expenses will be paid by The Academy.

To be invited to join The Academy is an honor that few students can share. So we know you will want to join us this spring.

We can promise you that it will be a thrilling, educational, and rewarding experience. We guarantee you will remember these two weeks for the rest of your life!

Yours truly,
Donald Marks
Director

Merrilee finished reading the letter over April's shoulder. "Wow," she murmured. "Is this for real?"

April shuffled through the other pages. "It all looks very official," she said. "I don't believe this! It's too amazing!"

Her heart was pounding. She glanced over the letter again. She had to grip it in two hands because her right hand was trembling.

"Two weeks on a tropical island? For free?" she said. "With all these incredible celebs. Whoa!"

"And maybe you'll come home with big bucks!" Merrilee exclaimed.

The two girls stared at each other openmouthed.

"This has got to be a joke," April said. "*No way* can this be real."

"When Pam finds out, she'll go starkraving berserk!" Merrilee said. "She'll freak out."

"I'll bet she was invited too," April replied, still gazing at the letter. "Pam's grades are better than mine. And she's a much better athlete. I wonder why I got picked."

"Don't put yourself down," Merrilee scolded. "Why are you always doing that?"

"I just wonder why they chose me," April said. "I'm quiet, I'm shy. I go camping with my family, but I'm not really an outdoors person." She gazed at the letter. "It's weird."

"It's not weird at all," Merrilee insisted. "You are such a hard worker. Your grades are just as good as Pam's. Maybe someone from The Academy saw you in *Bye Bye Birdie* last spring. You were fabulous!"

Merrilee giggled. "And you play *great* practical jokes!"

April laughed. "We really got Pam today—didn't we!"

"Call her!" Merrilee urged. "Go ahead. Call Pam. See if she got a letter too."

"You're kidding—right?" April shook her head. "No way I'm calling her."

The phone rang.

Both girls jumped.

April picked it up. "Hello?" Then she whispered to Merrilee, "It's Pam!"

"I knew it! She has a special radar," Merrilee whispered.

"April, I know what you and your friend Merrilee did to me in the lunchroom today," Pam said. "It took me a while, but I figured it out."

"Uh . . . well . . ." April muttered.

"I'll bet Merrilee is standing right there with you," Pam said bitterly. "And the two of you are still having a good laugh."

17

"No. We're not laughing," April replied. "Really."

"That was *so* not funny," Pam said.

"It was a *little* funny," April insisted. "You have to admit—"

"I try to be your friend," Pam said. "Because my mom says I have to. But it isn't easy, April. I don't know what your problem is. But—"

"Did you get a letter?" April blurted out.

"Excuse me? A letter?"

"Yes," April replied. "In the mail today. Did you get a letter from something called The Academy?"

"No," Pam said. "Why?"

"No reason," April replied. "Gotta go. See you tomorrow."

She clicked off the phone. Then she pumped her fist in the air. "Yesssss! Pam didn't get invited!"

A grin spread over Merrilee's face. "Think she'll be a little jealous when she finds out?"

April's eyes flashed. "Maybe a little."

Merrilee's grin faded. "Of course, there is just one problem, April. Your parents."

April narrowed her eyes at her friend. "What about my parents?"

"They're so strict," Merrilee replied. "What if they say no? They're always so worried about safety. Remember, they wouldn't let you go to Great Adventures last summer? What if they don't let you go to this?"

"They *have* to!" April exclaimed. "It's the chance of a lifetime! It—it's incredible! It's two weeks on a tropical island with other kids and dozens of celebs! And a chance to win thousands of dollars!"

"Whoa. Easy, girl—" Merrilee said.

"They can't say no!" April shouted. "Come *on*, Merrilee. They've got to let me go. They've *got* to! It's a tiny little island with no one else living on it. What could go wrong? Tell me—*what could go wrong?*"

Part Two
The Year 1680

Ravenswoode, a Tiny English Village

"Witch! Witch!"

"Kill the witch!"

Deborah Andersen screamed as she ran, trying to drown out the boys' ugly shouts. Her heavy black shoes pounded on the dirt path as it curved past the mill. She had to hold her long black skirt high in order to run from the boys who chased her. The coarse fabric felt heavy in her hands. Thorny vines tore at her ankles, ripping her woolen stockings.

"Witch! Be gone, witch!"

"Stop her before she flies away!"

A rock whirred past her head. "Noooo!" Deborah cried, ducking. The rock hit a tree with a sharp *clop* and bounced across the path. Deborah kept running.

The dirt path ended at the Fieldings' farm. Deborah stumbled across the fields, through the high clumps of grass and heather. The boys were not far behind. Around her the barley crop lay unharvested, black and rotting. A few bony cows stared wearily as Deborah ran by.

Did the people of Ravenswoode blame Deborah for the crop failures that spring? Did they blame her for the fat black insects that came swarming from inside the sweetcorn husks? For the purple worms that left the apples dead and shriveled on the tree? For the starving cows who gave only a thin stream of sour milk?

Yes. They did.

"I'M NOT A WITCH!" she wailed.

But the boys chased after her. Another rock sailed past her head.

"Fly away, witch!"

"Sprout blackbird wings and fly away!"

I wish I *could* fly away, Deborah thought bitterly. Away from these ignorant villagers who blame me for all their troubles.

She longed to get away from the cold village, away from the staring eyes, from the long, wet winters without enough firewood to warm her small cottage. Away from the farms and their scraggly crops. Away from the broken-down mill that seldom had any wheat to grind.

She wished she could leave behind the red-faced boys with their cruel taunts. The farmers and villagers with their accusing stares. The pale women in their dingy white bonnets, whispering when she walked by.

Gasping for breath, she glanced back. The boys still followed her, shaking their fists.

"Catch the witch!"

"Don't let her escape!"

Running hard, Deborah turned at the Fieldings' farmhouse. The brown grass sloped up toward the village with its thatched cottages and stone-and-shingle barns. Her cottage—and safety—stood on the other side of town.

Chickens clucked and wobbled at the Fieldings' door. A skinny rooster watched from the wall of the stone well. The well bucket lay on its side on the ground in a mound of yellow chicken feed.

A rock bounced hard off Deborah's shoulder. It sent a sharp jolt of pain down her side.

"Leave me be!" With a burst of fury, she spun around to face her pursuers. They caught up to her, breathing hard, and surrounded her.

Rubbing her shoulder, she stumbled, trying to escape. But she slipped in the grass and fell to her knees.

The circle of boys closed in on her. Five of them, she saw, in their gray school costumes. Gray coats over white muslin shirts and brown vests. Knee-length knickerbockers with white stockings and black buckled shoes. Not the finest clothes in the world, but far finer than any Deborah had ever owned.

Long tangles of greasy hair fell to the boys' shoulders. They drew short, heavy breaths, their faces red, their eyes narrow, suspicious, and alert. Deborah felt like a fox surrounded by hounds—and doomed to be torn to pieces by them.

Near the cottage, the chickens clucked and clattered in the Fieldings' yard. The only other sound was the whisper of spring wind through the stand of silver birch trees that bordered the farm.

Fly away now, Deborah ordered herself. *Fly away, blackbird, and scare the nasty boys.*

But she knew she hadn't the power.

Still on her knees, she pulled herself into a tight ball as the boys closed in on her. She clenched every muscle and gritted her teeth, steeling herself for the blows.

Two of the boys gripped slate-colored rocks. The others raised tight fists. Silent now, they moved nearer.

Deborah held up a hand, shielding her face.

"What are you going to do to me?" she whispered. "Please—what are you going to do?"

They stared down at her, eyes cold as stone. Bodies tensed, ready for a fight, they didn't say a word.

Why hadn't the boys hit her yet? Were they cowards?

Her heart pounding, Deborah climbed slowly to her feet. She smoothed the front of her long skirt.

Can I stare them down? Can I?

Can I pretend to give them the evil eye?

"Leave the village, witch!" The boy named Johnny Goodmann finally found his voice. Lanky and thin, with a long, pointed beak of a nose.

"Leave the village," Johnny's younger brother William echoed.

"I . . . live . . . here," Deborah replied slowly, keeping her eyes on them. Tensed for their sudden attack.

"But you are a witch," Aaron Harrison sneered. His long, wavy blond hair glowed in the late afternoon sunlight as if on fire. "You've brought a plague to this village. The crops were ruined because of your evil. My father said so."

"Your father is wrong," Deborah muttered. "I am just a girl."

Aaron laughed, cold and hard. "You don't act like one."

"Why do you try to go to school?" Johnny demanded. "What strange kind of girl are you, who sneaks into the schoolhouse to hear our lessons?"

"I—I want to learn," Deborah whispered. "I want to read as you do."

They all laughed now.

"Why should a girl read?" Aaron asked. "To read your evil spell books?" He grabbed her by the shoulder and shoved her hard.

Deborah stumbled backward, into Will Goodmann.

He cried out as if touched by flames.

At the well, the scraggly rooster crowed. The hens started to squawk.

Deborah caught her balance and spun around to face them. "I shall turn you all into chickens!" she shouted. "All! You will bend to me and peck the ground at my feet!"

"You *are* a witch!" Aaron gasped. "She admitted it!"

The rock fell from Johnny's hand.

Deborah pulled the hem of her skirt up to her ankles and started to run.

She expected them to follow her, to drag her

down. To use their rocks and fists as they had planned.

But to her surprise, they stood frozen like scarecrows. They watched her run and didn't take up the chase.

She kept glancing back as she made her way past the cottages at the edge of the village. Soon the boys were out of sight.

They *believed* me, she realized.

They believe I have the power to change them into clucking chickens.

Hot tears rolled down her face as she ran through the village square. In front of the meeting hall, she saw a blur of men in black. Alderman Harrison, Aaron's father, was talking to two of the village elders.

All three men turned to watch Deborah as she ran past.

Through the small market she ran, past the sad carts with their meager wares. A few jars of honey. A bucket or two of thin milk. A slab of rancid, dried beef. She ran across a wide, flat field toward the small, square cottage where she lived with her parents.

Wiping the tears from her cheeks with both hands, Deborah burst into the cottage. Katherine, her mother, turned from the hearth, where she was boiling a pot of large brown eggs.

"Why are you crying?" Katherine asked. "What is wrong, Moon Child?"

"Do not call me that, Mother!" Deborah wailed.

Katherine brushed back her daughter's light brown hair. The blue birthmark on Deborah's right temple came into view. The small, perfect crescent. The blue sliver of a moon.

"I have always called you Moon Child," Katherine murmured. "You were born under a crescent moon, Deborah, just like the one on your forehead."

"And I have been cursed by it!" Deborah declared angrily. "The villagers blame me for all their troubles. And all because of this mark on my face."

She brushed her mother's hand away and covered the blue crescent again with her hair. "The boys from the school—they chased me again."

"I heard them shouting," her mother replied. "I am so sorry, my girl."

Deborah made no attempt to stop the tears from streaking down her cheeks. "I—I am not a witch! I am only twelve years old. Why do they taunt me? Why do they all hate me so?"

Katherine returned to the hearth and threw a few more logs on the fire. "So many strange things have happened in the village since the day you were born." She stirred the eggs with a long wooden ladle.

"A two-headed calf was born the same day as you," Katherine continued. "And soon after paying a visit to our house, Councilman Forrester pulled two live mice from his ears. He has been deaf ever since. So many strange things. The villagers just don't know whom to blame."

Deborah sat on a stool by the fire. "Aaron Harrison torments me the most," she said. She clenched her fists so tightly, her fingernails dug into her palms. "He struts around with his blond hair like a prince. He leads the other boys against me."

"Try to calm yourself, Deborah," her mother urged. "I have fresh eggs for dinner and a loaf of bread from the market. Go to the well and wash your face. The cool water will help stop your tears."

Deborah ignored her suggestion. "If only I could pay those boys back, Mother. If only I could pay Aaron Harrison back for . . . for . . ." A sob escaped her throat.

"Hush, Deborah," Katherine whispered.

But Deborah couldn't hold back her fury. "How *dare* they throw stones at me! How *dare* they call me a witch! I hate those boys! I hate them! I . . . I wish I could make that horrible Aaron as unhappy as I am!"

The next morning, she got her wish.

The next morning dawned gray and chilly for spring. Katherine served breakfast in silence—cold eggs left over from the night before and steaming cups of herb tea.

Deborah hadn't slept all night. She couldn't erase Aaron and the other boys from her mind.

She sat at the rough wooden table and choked down an egg. The tea felt warm and soothing on her throat.

A blast of wind made the cottage walls shake. "Did you sleep, Mother?" Deborah asked.

Katherine shrugged. "A little." She sipped her tea and glanced at her daughter. "I see the heather is finally in bloom."

Deborah forced a smile. She had always loved the fresh purple heather in springtime.

Katherine squeezed Deborah's hand. "Let's go up the hill this morning and gather baskets of heather. We will fill the cottage with it."

Deborah nodded. "That's a wonderful idea,

Mother. The sweet-smelling heather will cheer me up."

They picked up straw baskets from the shed behind the cottage. Then they started across the field arm in arm.

The rising sun burned through the chill of the morning fog. The grass sparkled from the dew.

They had nearly reached the village square when they heard the sharp cry of voices. They spun around to see a line of four women running toward them, their aprons flapping.

"Katherine Andersen—hold your daughter there!" a woman shouted angrily. "Do not let her escape."

The basket fell from Deborah's hand. A wave of cold fear swept over her. "Mother, what is this about?"

Katherine gripped her daughter's hand and stared as the women furiously approached.

Deborah recognized Emily Harrison, Aaron's mother, her blond hair flying from under her dark blue bonnet. Her round face was red and stained with tears. Behind her came Rosemary Platt and two Platt cousins.

Emily ran up to Deborah and Katherine, breathing hard, her apron ruffling in the wind. "Witch!" she spat at Deborah. "Why did you do it? Why did you cast a spell on my poor son?"

Her eyes burned with fury. Deborah shrank back from her, afraid.

"You have done your last evil magic in this village!" Rosemary Platt roared.

"Magic—?" Deborah replied weakly.

Sobbing, Emily grabbed Deborah roughly by the arm. "Come with me," she seethed. "Come reverse your evil spell—at once!"

Deborah jerked her arm hard, trying to break free of Emily's tight grasp. But the women had her surrounded.

"I do not know what this is about!" she cried.

"Let go of my daughter!" Katherine shouted.

Emily Harrison pulled Deborah across the grass. "You will fix what you have done—or you will suffer for it. I will make sure of it."

Forming a tight, angry circle, the women herded Deborah and Katherine across the field, through the village square. A small crowd had gathered near the marketplace. They watched in silence as the four women dragged Deborah and her mother to the doorstep of the Harrison cottage. Freshly whitewashed, the Harrisons' house was two stories tall, the largest in the village.

"You have poisoned my home," Emily cried, tears pouring down her face. "You have infected my good home with your filthy evil! I demand that you reverse your spell and save my only son!"

What does she think I have done? Deborah wondered. What is she accusing me of?

What has happened to Aaron?

Emily Harrison pulled open the wooden cottage

33

door and shoved Deborah inside. "Aaron, I have brought her!" the furious woman shouted. "All will be well now!"

Trembling, her heart racing, Deborah squinted into the gloom of the cottage.

It took a short while to spot him, standing on the flat gray stones in front of the hearth.

And when Deborah finally recognized Aaron, she opened her mouth and began to scream.

The chicken took a few steps toward her. Its claws clicked on the stone floor.

Deborah raised her hands to the sides of her face and gaped in horror. Aaron's mother sobbed anew at the sight of her son.

The chicken had long, wavy blond hair. Aaron's hair.

It tilted its head and gazed up at Deborah with one flat black eye. It uttered a long, low *cluck* and stared at her without moving, accusing her.

Deborah struggled to catch her breath.

"We know this is your doing, Deborah," Emily Harrison whispered. "You threatened the boys yesterday. You promised to turn them into chickens. Aaron told me."

She shoved Deborah toward the long-haired chicken. "Now change him back. Change him back into our son. I'm begging you—if you have a drop of decency in your black heart . . ." She glared at Deborah, her eyes filling with tears.

35

"B-but . . ." Deborah struggled to choke out words. In spite of her hatred for Aaron, she felt sorry for him and his mother. "I did not do this," she whispered. "Believe me. I am innocent. I do not know any spells. I have no powers. I did not do this to Aaron."

The blond-haired chicken clucked again and scratched its beak against the stone floor.

"You must believe my daughter," Katherine spoke up. "She is telling the truth. She is innocent."

"Innocent?" Emily raged. "Innocent?" She grabbed Deborah's brown hair and tugged it back from her forehead.

"There is the crescent mark of the witch! Plain as day!" the woman shrieked. "Innocent? Innocent? With the mark of the moon on her face? With all the evil that has cursed this village since the day she was born?"

Deborah heard footsteps approach the doorway. Low voices.

She turned to see Alderman Harrison stride into the room, followed by two other men carrying muskets.

Harrison removed his tall black hat and stared in shock at the rooster, as if he still couldn't believe his eyes. Then he turned to Deborah.

"Your evil has no place in my home," he said in a trembling voice. "My son—my poor boy. Change him back, witch—or suffer the consequences."

"I—I do not know how," Deborah stammered. "Please, believe me—"

Harrison narrowed his eyes at her and scowled.

"I have brought the sheriff from the next village," he announced to everyone in the room. "Since this is Sunday, we cannot act. But I promise—Deborah Andersen will be hanged as a witch at nightfall tomorrow."

With a horrified cry, Deborah dropped to her knees. "Please, sir. I pray you. Have mercy. I did not do this."

"Spare my daughter's life," Katherine pleaded. "She has no powers, I swear!" She pulled Deborah to her feet.

"She has the mark of the moon on her head," Emily Harrison said. "She has brought nothing but despair to our village—more with every year of her life. We cannot tolerate her evil ways any longer!"

The woman bent down and lifted the blond-haired chicken into her arms. She raised it to Deborah's face. "Bring Aaron back! Reverse the curse you have cast on our son!"

Deborah shied away from the ugly animal. "I—I have no powers," she whispered.

"She is a liar!" Emily declared. She dropped the chicken and rushed at Deborah, shrieking, sobbing, scratching at Deborah's face, wrenching her hair.

Deborah shrank back. She raised her hands to shield her face.

Alderman Harrison grabbed his wife and struggled to tug her away. He held her in his arms. She sobbed on his shoulder.

"Go home," the alderman snapped at Katherine. "Take your daughter home for one last night. The village council will meet tomorrow morning. Their sentence will be carried out at dusk."

"I beg you," Katherine said. "Spare my daughter's life. She is only twelve. Show mercy, sir. I will take her away from the village if you let her live."

"Leave now," Harrison sneered, waving them toward the door. "The council will decide your daughter's fate. Her punishment will be harsh—and final."

"Please—!" Deborah cried.

Her mother pulled her to the cottage door. The last thing Deborah saw before stumbling out into the daylight was the long-haired chicken, its chest heaving in and out as it gazed up at her with one flat black eye.

Deborah spent the rest of the day in a daze, pacing back and forth in the small cottage. Her mother prepared a small supper of day-old bread and a bit of mutton stew. Deborah sat at the table on her straw-seated chair and stared at the food on her plate. She couldn't touch her dinner, even though she knew it might be her last.

Her mother spoke little. After supper, Deborah washed the dented pewter dishes. Katherine sat in a corner facing the hearth with a small prayer book in her lap. She kept her head bowed. She stayed there all evening, not once looking up.

Deborah had never seen her mother pray before.

Finally, after changing into her linen nightshirt, Deborah sat beside her mother near the dying fire. "Will they hang me, Mother?" she asked. "Will they?"

Katherine lowered her prayer book. "They are honorable men. They will come to their senses," she replied in a dry, flat voice.

Deborah swallowed hard. She felt chilled under her heavy nightshirt. She hugged herself to stop trembling. "Mother, you never asked me if I did cast that spell on Aaron Harrison. You never asked if I have powers that I use on the villagers."

The embers crackled in the hearth. Katherine gazed at Deborah for a long time. "I have no need to ask," she said finally. "I know my daughter. I know that you are not a witch."

Deborah wrapped her arms around her mother and buried her face in her neck. She wanted her mother to tell her that everything would be okay. That her life would be spared. That the villagers would realize their mistake.

But Katherine remained grim-faced, staring into the dying fire. She is holding back tears, Deborah thought. She is forcing herself not to cry in front of me.

Deborah lay on her straw bed but couldn't sleep. Is this my last night on earth? she wondered.

She stared up at the darkness. Pictures rolled through her mind. Her father with all of his bundled wares, turning to wave to her as he left for the trading ship that would take him to China . . . Aaron and the other boys chasing her from the school, throwing rocks and calling her names . . . The blond rooster staring up at her, accusing her . . .

Deborah finally drifted off to sleep. But shouts and cries from outside the cottage shook her awake. Her first thought: *They are coming for me!*

She jumped from bed and ran to the front room. The cottage door was open. Katherine stood in the doorway, staring out. Her face and nightshirt reflected a flashing, flickering red glow.

In the distance, the alarmed shouts grew louder.

"Mother—" Deborah gasped. "What is happening?"

Deborah rushed to the doorway and pressed up beside her mother.

She stared at the bright red flames that danced up to the night sky. A roaring blaze. People ran in all directions, waving wildly, screaming. A dog barked frantically in the distance.

The roar of the fire nearly drowned out the shrieks and cries.

A wall of flames shot up over the buildings across the field. The crackle of burning wood rang out over the thunder of the fire. Thick clouds of smoke billowed over the flames.

"The village burns," Katherine murmured. Deborah saw the flames reflected in her mother's eyes.

"But—how?" Deborah whispered.

Men ran in panic. Women held their children close, shrieking in terror.

Without realizing what she was doing, Deborah began to wander across the field toward the burning village. Bathed in red, she thought. Everyone is bathed in red, as if they've been dipped in the fire.

She shivered as she drew nearer. A cold wind blew back her hair. The wind carried the choking aroma of the smoke. And as it brushed Deborah's arms, the smoke felt colder than the air.

Cold?

Yes. The wind off the flames was cold.

But how could that be?

As Deborah wandered closer, she could make out the frightened words of the villagers. . . .

"Cold! The flames are cold!"

"The fire burns cold! What kind of flames are these?"

"The fire freezes as it burns!"

"Witchcraft! Witchcraft!"

Deborah's heart stopped. She spun around. Started to run back to her cottage.

Too late.

She saw the accusing stares of the villagers. Saw the fright, the hatred in their eyes as they glared at her.

Saw their anger.

I'm doomed, she thought, running over the grass, the ground flashing red beneath her feet.

I didn't make this strange, cold fire. But it has sealed my fate.

They will come for me now. They will not let me live.

• • •

They came for Deborah the next morning.

The whole village gathered behind Alderman

Harrison and the two men carrying muskets. They stood in grim-faced silence as the alderman led Deborah and her mother from the cottage.

Across the field, the fire still sizzled. Black smoke choked the morning sky, blocking the sun, making it as dark as dusk.

Slabs of ice covered the ground where the houses and cottages and village buildings had stood. The strange, cold fire had left a blanket of ice over the ashes.

The entire village was in ruins. There was nothing left.

The villagers, exhausted, stood in silence. Alderman Harrison stepped close to Deborah, his shadow falling over her like a shroud.

"You have cursed the village of Ravenswoode for the last time," he announced in a booming voice.

"No! Spare my daughter!" Katherine shrieked. "I beg you! Spare her!"

Deborah's legs began to tremble. She wondered if she would be able to stand. The ground tilted. She suddenly felt dizzy and dazed.

The alderman stared somberly at her. "Because your mother is a good and honest woman, your life will be spared," he announced. "But we will suffer no more of your evil magic."

Deborah uttered a shuddering moan. She gripped her mother's hand, surprised to find it as icy as hers.

"You must leave the village at once," Harrison ordered. "You must leave and never return. You will be taken to the town of Plymouth. There you will board a sailing ship. The ship will carry you to a distant island—a tropical island where no people live."

"But, sir—" Deborah began to protest.

"You are sentenced to live the rest of your life alone, Deborah Andersen!" Harrison's voice rang out. "All alone on an island that no one else will ever visit. Alone, where you cannot harm anyone with your witchcraft."

Deborah reached out her hands to beg him to change his mind. But Harrison spun away from her. He and the two men with muskets strode away. The villagers followed, returning to the frozen ashes of their town.

Deborah realized she was still gripping her mother's hand. Katherine had a strange, distant smile on her face. A sad, joyless smile, Deborah realized.

"They spared your life," Katherine said softly.

"But, Mother—" Deborah protested. "What kind of a life will I lead all alone forever on a distant, empty island? Must I really spend the rest of my life there? What can I do, Mother? *What can I do?*"

Part Three

A Tropical Island This Spring

April leaned on the deck railing of the boat and gazed out at the island. She saw tilting palm trees along the shore and behind them, green hills gleaming under the golden sunlight.

It's like make-believe, she thought. The gentle waves of pale, aqua water . . . the shimmering blue rocks on the shoreline . . . the small white cabins half-hidden in the tangled trees . . .

Were those caves cut into the blue rocks? I'd love to go exploring in caves, April thought.

She tugged at the red plastic earring dangling from her left ear. It's like a movie set! She told herself. I can't believe this is happening to me!

The pilot gunned the motor, and the boat lifted up as it roared over the top of the water. A short wooden dock came into view. Small white motorboats bobbed in the water.

April could see two people dressed in white shorts and T-shirts running along the shore to meet the boat. The kids on the deck behind her called out and waved to them.

April turned to Kristen Wood and flashed her a thumbs-up.

"We made it!" Kristen exclaimed in her hoarse, raspy voice.

Three other Academy kids had come on the boat ride from the main island. April and Kristen had become instant friends.

Kristen was short and wiry, a bundle of energy. She had raven black hair pulled back tight behind her head. Dark, round eyes. Intense eyes that seemed to stare right through you. And that funny hoarse voice.

A girl named Martine was tall and blond and had a big, throaty laugh. She said she was an all-state swimmer back home in California. She hoped to spend a lot of time swimming around the island.

The third kid was a red-haired boy named Anthony. April thought he seemed nervous, very tense and serious. He didn't like to be teased about his freckles. And he didn't join in any of their jokes. While the others hung out and enjoyed the sun, Anthony stayed down below and read a book.

"I wonder if the famous people are here already," April said. "Can you believe we're going to hang out with movie stars, prizewinning scientists, and a Supreme Court justice?"

Martine's blond hair fluttered in the wind. "Maybe we'll all be discovered and get big movie contracts," she said.

Kristen laughed. "Dream a lot?" she asked Martine.

The pilot cut the motor, and the boat slowed, drifting to the dock. Two young men stood waiting to greet the boat. Their T-shirts had bold black type across the front: ACADEMY STAFF.

The pilot tossed out the rope. One of the young men caught it and tied it to the pole.

April's heart started to race. I'm here, she thought. I'm actually here. This is going to be the most amazing two weeks of my life.

"Hey, guys—how's it going?" One of the young men leaned down and took Martine's hand. He helped pull her onto the wood-planked deck. "Welcome to the Academy village. I'm Josh—and that ugly guy over there is Rick."

"Give me a break," Rick muttered.

April reached up her hand and Josh helped her out of the boat. He has a great smile, she thought.

Josh was tanned and had olive green eyes and a thick mop of wavy, unbrushed black hair.

Next, he helped pull Kristen up. Anthony insisted on climbing out without any help.

"Two . . . three . . . four . . ." Rick pointed at the kids as he counted. He turned to Josh. "Hey, weren't we expecting only three? How come there are four of you?"

"One of us is a stowaway," Kristen joked.

Josh and Rick didn't laugh. "This is definitely weird," Josh said.

Rick shrugged. "Whatever. We'll let Marks sort it out."

"Donald Marks is our grand and glorious leader," Josh announced. "That's his royal castle over there." He pointed to a white shack at the edge of the trees. "Rick and I are his humble slaves."

Rick gave Josh a playful shove. "Actually, Marks is a pretty good guy," he said. "He put this whole thing together. He's really impressive. You'll see. You're going to meet him now."

"What about our bags?" Anthony asked.

"We slaves will unload them," Josh replied. "When you get your team assignment, we'll bring them around to your cabin."

Anthony frowned. "Team assignment? You mean we have to be on teams?"

Josh nodded. "For the Life Games."

"Believe me, when the games begin, you'll be glad to have teammates," Rick said.

Anthony doesn't seem like much of a team player, April thought. Maybe he's just nervous. Like me. Just the same, I hope he isn't on my team.

She gazed around at the small village of shacks as Josh led them to Donald Marks. Several of them had thatched roofs of palm-tree leaves. A long, low building appeared to be a meeting hall.

Four boys were tossing a Frisbee around in a sandy clearing between the rows of shacks. April saw two girls stretched out on beach towels, catching some rays.

This is going to be like the best summer camp in the world! she thought.

A hand-painted sign on the door to Marks's office read BIG CHEESE. Josh pulled open the door and ushered April and the others inside.

Marks sat behind a table piled high with papers and folders. He jumped to his feet as they entered, sending a stack of folders toppling over the table.

"Welcome, welcome," he said, clasping his hands in front of him.

He's a giant! April thought.

Marks was so tall, he had to bend his head to keep from hitting the low ceiling. He had a huge head, round as a bowling ball and totally bald.

He had tiny black eyes above a bulby nose, and the dark stubble of a beard just started. He was big and wide, April saw, broad-shouldered, with bulging biceps poking out from under his massive ACADEMY STAFF T-shirt.

Like a wrestler, April thought. That's what he reminds me of. One of those enormous wrestlers on TV.

He welcomed them warmly, moving down the line of kids, shaking their hands. He has a wrestler's grip too, April thought. Her hand throbbed after Marks was finished shaking it.

"Well, we're all here," Marks said, beaming at them, his tiny eyes sparkling. "I know it was a long trip for you. But I think it will be worth it."

He began pawing through the papers on his desk. "You're all probably eager to get unpacked and relax a bit. Let me find your assignments here. . . ."

He looked up. "You're probably wondering why I don't have all this stuff on a computer. Well . . . we built a small electric generator here on the island. But we have to be careful how much power we use. So—no computers." He looked at Martine. "And no hair dryers."

"Are there lights in the camp at night?" April asked.

"A few," Marks replied, shuffling through the papers. "But it's pretty dark. Remember, no one has ever lived on this island. We had to build everything ourselves."

He pulled out a clipboard. "Ah-ha. Here it is. Now, let me just check off your names." Suddenly, his expression changed, and he blinked several times at the page on the clipboard.

"Whoa," he said. "That's weird." He squinted at the clipboard. "My eyes are playing tricks on me. The words are swimming on the page." He shook his head. "Guess I've been out in the sun too long. Or else I need glasses."

He turned back to the list of names. One by one, he checked off Anthony, Martine, and Kristen. Then he turned to April. "Last but not least," he said, grinning at her through the dark stubble of beard. "And what is your name?"

"April Powers."

He squinted at his checklist. "Powers . . . Powers . . ." He gazed up at April as if studying her. "April Powers . . ."

April nodded.

"April, did you get a letter from us? An invitation?" Marks asked.

April could feel her face growing hot. "Yes, of course," she answered sharply. She tugged tensely at her earring.

Marks ran his finger slowly down the long list of names on the clipboard. Then, scratching his bald head with one chubby hand, he turned back to April.

"I'm real sorry," he said softly. "But you're not on the list."

April felt her face grow hot again. "I—I don't understand," she said.

Marks frowned at his checklist. He ran his finger down the names once again, counting, moving his lips.

"Eleven . . . twelve. Yes, we already have twelve," he said. He squinted at April. "Did you bring your invitation by any chance?"

"Well . . . no," April replied. "I didn't think . . . "

"We have room for only twelve kids," Marks said, scratching the top of his head again. "And your name isn't on the list."

"But—how can that be?" April asked. She was trying to stay calm, but her voice broke.

Marks studied the checklist again. He flipped through several pages. "Could there be someone here who doesn't belong?" he muttered.

He dropped heavily into the canvas chair behind his desk. "Well, we can't have thirteen," he said, shaking his head. "We have three teams of four. And

only twelve beds. There's no room for a thirteenth."
He stared at April as if challenging her.

"Wh-what do you mean?" April stammered.

"You can't stay. We'll have to send you home,"
Marks said.

"But—I've come all this way!" April cried.

Kristen stepped up and put a hand on April's
shoulder. "This isn't fair," she said to Marks. "Maybe
April and I could share somehow. Maybe we could
work together or something."

That's so sweet of Kristen, April thought. I just
met her yesterday, and she is already being such a
good friend.

Marks shook his head again. "I'm sorry," he said.
"There is a hundred thousand dollars at stake here. I
cannot allow someone to stay who isn't on the list. It
would throw the games off entirely. And it wouldn't
be fair to the others."

"But—but—" April sputtered. She felt tears
welling in her eyes. She bit her lip to keep from crying.

This isn't right, she thought. This just isn't right.

I was invited. My name should be on that list.

Either Marks made a mistake. Or there's someone
here who doesn't belong.

But I was invited. I should be allowed to stay.

It isn't fair. It isn't fair.

What am I going to do?

A high scream behind her made April gasp. She
jumped in surprise.

And turned to see Martine open her mouth in another shrill scream.

"NOOOOO! HELP ME! OHHHH, HELP!"

Bright red blood spurted from Martine's ears. She spread her hands over her ears. But the blood squirted out in streams, like water from a water pistol.

"OHHHH, HELP. MY EARDRUMS . . ."

Martine dropped to her knees, screaming, crying. Blood sprayed the room. Her blond hair was soaked in it.

Marks moved quickly. He ran to the door and shouted for Josh and Nick. Then he removed a first aid kit from his desk drawer.

He dropped beside Martine and pulled her hands away from her ears. Balling up cotton gauze, he struggled to stop the flow of blood.

"Something is horribly wrong. Have your eardrums burst?" Marks cried. "Have you had ear trouble before?"

Martine shook her head. "No. Oh . . . they hurt! They *hurt*!" Martine wailed. "I—I can't *stand* it!"

Josh and Nick and a young, dark-haired woman burst into the doorway. Their eyes bulged in shock when they saw Martine down on the floor, and all the blood.

"Where is the nurse?" Marks demanded.

"On the main island," Rick replied.

"Well then, this girl has to be rushed to the main island," Marks ordered. "Get her in the boat. Take her—now."

The three staff members helped Martine to her feet. She was wailing and crying, pressing her hands to her ears. Gently, they guided her out of Marks's office.

Marks slumped into his chair with a long sigh. His bald head glistened with sweat. He had dried blood on his hands and down the front of his T-shirt.

April suddenly realized she'd been biting her bottom lip. She tasted blood as she loosened her jaw. Her heart pounded in her chest. She kept seeing the streams of bright blood shooting from Martine's ears.

How did that happen? she wondered. One minute Martine was standing here calmly.

And the next . . .

April turned and saw Marks staring at her. His forehead creased and his little, dark eyes burned into hers. As if he were studying her. Sizing her up.

Finally, he spoke. "I don't really understand what happened to Martine. It was so sudden. Can eardrums burst for no reason?"

"Poor Martine," Kristen whispered. "That was terrifying. All that blood."

"Whoa. It totally freaked me," Anthony said,

looking very pale, so pale, his freckles had disappeared. "I'm still shaking. I think I'm going to have nightmares tonight."

"The nurse on the main island will treat Martine," Marks said. "As soon as she is able to fly, we'll get her home."

Marks rubbed his stubbly cheeks. He squinted at April. "Well . . . I guess there is a place for you after all."

April swallowed. If only her heart would stop thudding so hard and fast. "You mean—?"

"We need twelve kids," Marks said. "Now you're number twelve. Martine is gone. So you can stay, April." He gazed down at the checklist on his desk. "Weird," he muttered.

"Thank you! Thank you!" April cried.

Marks told them to go outside and explore the camp. Meet the other kids. "I want to clean up this room," he said. "Then I'll come out to announce your cabin and team assignments."

April followed Kristen and Anthony out of the little shack into the sunlight. A million thoughts whirred through her mind, making her feel dizzy.

What happened in there? she wondered. Why wasn't my name on the list? Why did Marks stare at me so strangely? And why did Martine's eardrums burst for no reason?

It was so awful. So frightening.

April suddenly realized that Anthony was giggling. It was the first time she had ever seen him smile. "Anthony? What's so funny?" she asked.

Anthony blushed. "Nothing," he said. "Nothing." And he hurried away.

The rope bridge swayed in the warm breeze. Below the bridge, a narrow stream trickled softly, the water glinting in the sunlight.

That bridge is too flimsy to hold anyone, April thought. She felt a chill of fear. Are they really going to make us cross over it? The ropes are frayed and stretched.

April gazed at the single rope that formed a railing. And at the gaps in the bridge floor. If you miss a step, you could fall right through, she thought.

"This looks like fun!" Anthony said, stepping up beside her. He rubbed his hands together.

Is he kidding? April wondered. Ever since she saw him giggling after Martine's horrible ear problem, she couldn't figure him out.

Was he really eager to race across this flimsy rope bridge? Or was he making some kind of joke?

Anthony was so intense most of the time. And then something would strike him as funny, and he would start to giggle. But they were on the same team, so April had to try to get along with him.

The other two members of the team stepped up beside her. April was glad that Kristen had been assigned to her team. She and Kristen weren't very much alike. Compared to Kristen, April was quiet and thoughtful. And she wasn't much of an athlete.

Small and wiry, Kristen couldn't sit still. She had to be on the move. She was eager to compete. She wanted to win win win. And she never stopped talking.

The fourth team member was a boy named Marlin. He was African American, tall, and very athletic. Marlin had short hair, large brown eyes that always seemed to be taking everything in and sizing everyone up, a tiny silver ring in one ear, and a winning smile.

Marlin was always encouraging the other team members, cheering them on—a leader and a cheerleader at the same time. If we had a team captain, it should be Marlin, April thought.

The teams had been organized at the first Academy meeting the night April had arrived. Marks had greeted everyone at the door to the meeting lodge, shaking hands, slapping high-fives, laughing, chatting with everyone.

He introduced Josh, Rick, and Abby, his three staff members. And then Marks had the twelve kids stand up one by one, introduce themselves, and tell a little about their lives.

"We have three teams for our Life Games," Marks announced. "There will be many competitions. For most of the games, the winning team will get ten points. Second place will win five points. Third place wins zero.

"The most important competitions will be for loyalty, honesty, and bravery," he continued. "They are worth fifty points each. After each of these big competitions, the losing team will be eliminated."

"What does that mean exactly?" Dolores, a tall blond girl in a red midriff shirt asked from the back row.

"What does *eliminated* mean?" Marks replied. "It means you're *gone*. You're outta there!"

A few kids laughed. But most of them stared intently at Marks, their expressions solemn.

This is a serious group, April decided. They really came here to compete. And to win the hundred thousand dollars.

"Only one team will be left to face the bravery challenge," Marks continued. "And if they succeed, they will split the cash prize. I wish you all good luck. This is a beautiful island. But it holds many challenges."

"When will the celebs arrive?" Dolores called out. "Will they perform for us? Or just hang out?"

Marks slapped at a mosquito on his bald head. "We are busy scheduling their boat," he replied. "I hope to have an answer for you in a day or two. You will all have the excitement of getting to know these interesting and successful people very soon."

Anthony, sitting in the front row, raised his hand.

"Will the Life Games competitions begin first thing tomorrow?" he asked.

Marks shook his head. "They've already begun," he murmured.

"We're going to win this thing," Marlin declared after the meeting. He gathered Kristen, April, and Anthony together in the sandy square between the cabins. "No problem. We're going to win—big-time!"

And raising his hands high above his head, he started a chant. "We're going to win! We're going to win! We're going to win!"

Kristen and Anthony quickly joined in. April always felt awkward chanting with a crowd. She just wasn't the cheerleader type. But she saw the others staring at her, so she joined in too.

"We're going to win! We're going to win!" Now Marlin got them jumping as they chanted. And April quickly got into the spirit. She chanted and jumped with the others, feeling her excitement rise. Feeling good about being part of a team.

Walking to their cabins, the kids on the other two teams saw them—and quickly gathered to start their own chants.

"We're going to win! We're going to win!"

Louder. Louder. The voices rang out through the trees, echoed off the rocks, carried by the soft winds of the tiny island.

This is *intense*! April thought. Everyone is so *psyched*.

This should be an amazing two weeks!

Now, it was the next afternoon. April stared at the rope bridge, swaying in the wind.

It doesn't look like a bridge, she thought. It looks like a giant net. How are we supposed to *run* over those knotted ropes?

The stream below it isn't deep enough to swim in, she realized. If someone should fall off the bridge— or fall through it . . .

She suddenly found herself thinking about Pam back home. When April told her friend about The Academy, Pam had been totally jealous.

"I should have been invited," Pam had sneered. "Everyone knows I'm a much better athlete than you. I really like to win. You don't even care about stuff like that.

"There must have been some kind of mistake," Pam had said.

Those words had made April so angry, she could barely speak. She left for the island without saying good-bye to Pam.

I'm going to show Pam that she was wrong, April thought, staring at the rope bridge. Pam isn't the only one who likes to compete. I'm a winner too.

A shrill whistle shook April from her thoughts.

Josh was waving for everyone to come listen to him. He blew the whistle again.

Josh's wavy, dark hair fluttered in the wind. He was wearing a white ACADEMY STAFF T-shirt and baggy denim cutoffs. "Show time, everyone!" he called.

He pointed with his whistle to the rope bridge. "This is your first test," he announced. "Ten points for first place. Five points for second. Has anyone ever raced over a rope bridge before?"

No hands went up.

"Well, I'll give you the secret to crossing it," Josh said. "Don't look down!"

He meant that as a joke. But only a few kids snickered.

"This is a simple race," Josh announced. "I'll be timing each racer. One person runs across at a time. I'll add up the total team time. The team with the lowest total wins the race."

He gazed around the group of twelve kids. "Any questions? Everybody ready?"

He pulled out a silvery stopwatch. "Let's have Team One. Over here. You're first."

April's group was Team Three.

We'll get to watch the other two teams, April realized. That will give me plenty of time to get even *more* nervous!

The next few minutes were a blur of action.

The whistle blew. Gripping the rope railing, kids pulled themselves one by one across the swaying bridge.

Some kids ran easily, heads up, ignoring the swaying of the bridge and the creaking of the knotted ropes beneath them.

Others made their way more cautiously, taking it a step at a time. Making sure each foothold was secure before taking the next step.

Josh's whistle blew. Kids cheered. April tugged at her earring, watching the others compete. Can I do it? she wondered. She thought of Pam. *Yes, I can!*

"WHOOOOAAAA!"

Kids gasped as Ernie, a big, beefy guy on Team Two, slipped. His shoe caught on a rope, and he fell to his stomach on the swaying bridge floor. With a groan, Ernie grabbed the rope rail and pulled himself up quickly.

"Hurry, Ernie! Go! Go! Go!" His three teammates urged him on. He stumbled to the end of the bridge. The whistle blew. His teammates cheered and congratulated him.

Our turn, April thought. She took a deep breath. "Don't blow it," she muttered to herself.

"Anthony, go first," Marlin ordered. "Then Kristen, then me, then April. Good luck, guys. We can do it!"

At the whistle, Anthony took off. Leaning forward, he pulled himself quickly over the ropes, moving in a steady rhythm.

He made it easily to the other side, and Kristen raced onto the swaying bridge. She stumbled at first, but raised her knees high, and her sneakers moved easily from rope to rope.

April's heart started to pound as she watched Marlin make his run. We're doing great, she realized. We can win this race—if I don't mess up.

Marlin flew over the bridge. April moved into place, gripping the rope railing in her right hand. She realized she was gritting her teeth so hard, her jaw ached. Taking a deep breath, she forced her muscles to relax.

The whistle blew. April took off over the swaying bridge. "Go! Go! Go!" She could hear her teammates cheering her on.

Her legs trembled but caught a rhythm. She raised her eyes to see the others waving her in, shouting excitedly.

She was halfway across the bridge when she fell.

Her foot caught on a rope—and she felt her body hurtle forward.

The rope rail flew out of her hand. She stumbled to the side. Made a wild grab for the rope.

Missed.

I'm falling! she realized in that brief second of terror.

I'm falling over the side!

70

April landed hard on her stomach. The ropes bounced beneath her.

Stunned, she heard the shouts and screams from the end of the bridge. And realized she hadn't fallen over the side.

"Get up! Get up! Get up!" her teammates were pleading.

Shaking off her confusion, April climbed to her feet. The end of the bridge still appeared a mile away. Her legs trembling, she started to run again.

Go! Go! Go! she urged herself. I can do it! I can!

And now she felt as if she were flying, flying over the swaying ropes.

Josh's whistle blew as she dove to the other side. "Yesssss!" She dropped to her knees, grateful to be on solid ground.

"Team One is our winner—by six seconds!" Josh announced. "Team Two takes second place."

April watched the members of the winning teams celebrate, jumping up and down, cheering and congratulating one another.

As she started to climb to her feet, Marlin and Anthony stepped in front of her.

"What was your *problem*?" Anthony demanded angrily. "Did you know it was a *race*?"

"Give her a break," Marlin said. He pushed Anthony back. "She slipped, that's all."

"But what were you doing down there? Taking a nap?" Anthony demanded.

"That's not fair," Kristen said sharply, glaring at Anthony. "We're all going to mess up sometime."

"But we've got to be a *team*," Marlin added. "We've got to stick together. We'll get them next time."

Anthony balled his hands into fists. His normally pale face was bright red. "We have to win!" he seethed. "My family really needs this money!"

"Calm down," Kristen told him. "We're going to win. I know it."

"Just shape up," Anthony snapped at April. "You weren't even supposed to be here!"

April jumped back as if she'd been slapped. Anthony's remark really stung.

Did everyone think the way he did? Did they all believe she didn't belong?

"Don't listen to him," Kristen said, putting an arm around April's shoulders. "He has a bad temper. I guess he can't help it. He's a redhead."

For some reason, that made April laugh. She and Kristen followed the others back toward the Academy village.

They followed the dirt path through the thick island forest. Birds chirped in the trees. Broad palm leaves scraped and scratched overhead. Tiny brown lizards scampered over the path.

"You'll probably beat everyone at the rock climbing thing tomorrow," Kristen said.

The rock climbing competition.

April had forgotten that was the next event. It was going to be held at those strange blue rocks on the shore. The shimmering blue hills of rocks April had seen from the boat.

I want to do well in that competition, she told herself. I *have* to do well.

As they made their way to the village, she saw Anthony watching her.

How can I show Anthony that I'm a winner too? she wondered. How can I show everyone that I belong on this team?

She stared at the blue rocks. Shimmering like ice, they seemed to be calling to her, inviting her, drawing her toward them.

Yes, she thought. Yes. I know what I'm going to do.

After lunch, most of the other kids headed to the beach for a swim. April made her way along the curving shore to the outcropping of rocks.

I'm going to practice, she decided. I'm going to climb the rocks today and get a good feel for them.

I'm not going to be the one to mess up tomorrow.

The afternoon sun beamed down from straight overhead. April had a baseball cap pulled down over her hair. But she could feel the back of her neck burning. She sighed, remembering that she had intended to bring sunscreen.

She wore a pale-blue sleeveless T-shirt and white tennis shorts. Oh, well, she thought. I'm going to get a little sunburned today.

The rocks rose up in front of her like small mountains. They glowed under the bright sun. Waves lapped against the bottom of the stone walls, then retreated.

The wet rocks are going to be slippery, April thought. She stepped off the sandy shore onto pebbly stones. A few more steps and she stood in the shadow of the steeply sloping rocks.

She could see dark caves cut into the rock face. The jagged openings looked like the cave doors in cartoons.

What kind of stone is this? she wondered. I've never seen blue rocks before.

A flash of color caught her eye.

Something moved quickly—in one of the caves?

April squinted hard, shielding her eyes from the bright sunlight. Was it a bird? Some kind of sea creature using the cave as shelter?

Whatever it was had vanished.

She took a deep breath, leaned forward, and started to climb the rocks. To her surprise, she felt a puff of cold air.

Her sneakers slid over the slippery rock surface. She reached for the slab of rock at her shoulders to hoist herself up.

"Whoa!" April cried out in surprise.

The rock—it was *cold*.

April slid her hands over the rocks all around. Yes. They were cold. And the air around them carried a chill.

But how could that be? The sun was beaming down so strong. April's shoulders were already burned pink.

These rocks were under the hot sun every day. How could they stay so cold?

April pulled herself up onto a ledge. The big flat

stones sloped up gently. She could run across them easily.

Sunlight glowed off the rock surface. But she could feel the cold rising off the stones as she made her way up the slope.

Near the top, she turned and looked back. She had climbed higher than she had thought.

Down below, sparkling blue-green ocean waves lapped gently at the rocks on the shore. Far to the left, she could see kids swimming in the water.

It's so beautiful here, April thought.

She turned back in time to see another flash of color in a cave opening.

And then something else caught her eye. Something piled on the rocks just outside the cave.

She scrambled over the sloping slick surface. And knelt down beside the pile of white objects.

Bones?

Yes. Delicate fish and bird bones were stacked in a tall pile that formed a perfect circle.

April studied the pile, then gazed around at the cave mouths cut into the rocks all around.

How did these bones get up here? she wondered.

Did an animal carry its prey up here to devour it in safety? Is this the secret eating place of some kind of island creature?

She stared at the bones. All picked clean.

An animal wouldn't stack up bones so perfectly— would it? she wondered.

Another thought gave her a shiver. She turned and stared at the caves.

Is someone else living on this island?

"But the bones were in a perfect circle," April explained.

Marlin shrugged his broad shoulders. "So? What does that prove?"

"An animal couldn't do that," April insisted. "It proves that we're not alone on this island. There's someone else here."

Her three teammates shook their heads.

They were sitting on the sand, near the shore. A red ball of a sun was sinking slowly into the ocean, filling the water with a spectacular light show.

Seagulls glided lazily in the graying sky. Two tall white herons strutted up and down the beach, ignoring the four kids and their argument.

"I don't understand why you don't believe me," April said. "I mean—"

"Marks told us that no one has ever lived on this island," Anthony interrupted. "So why do you want to call him a liar?"

"I don't. I'm not saying he's a liar. But maybe he

doesn't know everything about this island."

"How could anyone live on this island?" Kristen chimed in. "It's impossible. There is absolutely nothing here. I think you should forget about those bones, April."

"But—" April started to protest.

"What if Marks put those bones there?" Marlin asked.

"Yes. Right!" Anthony quickly agreed. "What if it's part of a test? You know, one of the Life Games."

"What if the bones are part of the loyalty test?" Marlin continued. "And you are ruining it for us by calling Marks a liar."

"You are going to mess it up for us *again*!" Anthony said, glaring at April.

April felt herself losing control. "What is your *problem*, Anthony?" she demanded. "You've been on my case ever since we arrived."

His cheeks turned bright red. "Sorry," he muttered. "Really. Guess I'm just losing it or something." He stuck out his hand. "Shake?"

April shook his hand. She smiled at him. "Friends?"

"Sure," he said.

Everyone here is so totally tense, April thought. All of us. We should be laughing and kidding around. It should be nonstop party time on this amazing island.

But everyone is totally stressed about the Life Games competitions. No one can relax.

Maybe I can do something about that, she thought. Maybe I can do something to get everyone to lighten up and have a few laughs. . . .

The next morning, high clouds covered the sky. A cool wind from the ocean blew over the village. The boats bobbed roughly in the choppy waves at the dock. The wind made the trees creak and groan.

April hurried along the row of cottages to catch up to her three teammates. They were making their way into the mess hall for breakfast.

"Hey, wait up!" April called. "I'll show you a cool magic trick."

The four of them stopped in the doorway of the mess hall. Several kids were already seated at the two long wooden tables. April spotted Dolores in the center of the room, heading to the food table against the wall.

April grinned at her teammates. "Check this out. Watch what I can make Dolores do."

She raised her right hand, pointed her finger at Dolores, and mumbled some words to herself.

In the middle of the room, Dolores suddenly stopped. Her eyes went wide. Her mouth dropped open. And she let out a loud *cluck*.

April waved her hand at Dolores, and Dolores began strutting around the room, clucking like a chicken.

Some cried out in surprise. Soon everyone was laughing.

Perfect, April thought. Everyone is enjoying my little magic act. "Now, watch this," she called out.

April pointed at Dolores and mumbled some more nonsense words.

Across the room, Dolores's body went stiff. And then she began to spin. Slowly at first, her arms dangling loosely at her sides.

Her long, blond hair whirled in the air as she spun faster. Her arms rose as if trying to keep her balance. "Help me!" Dolores wailed in horror. "Somebody—help me!"

The laughter stopped. The room grew silent. All eyes were on the tall, spinning girl.

Dolores spun faster, her hair whipping around her. She uttered scream after scream.

Just as we rehearsed, April thought.

She kept her finger pointed at Dolores and narrowed her eyes, pretending to concentrate her powers on her.

Dolores is a great screamer, April thought. She really sounds terrified!

When I asked her to help me with this little joke last night, she didn't want to do it. She didn't think she would be good at it. But she's terrific!

April gazed around the mess hall. Kids were silent, gaping in wide-eyed horror. Beside her, Kristen hugged herself tightly, her dark eyes locked on the spinning girl. Marlin and Anthony kept staring from Dolores to April.

They're buying it, April thought gleefully. They really believe I'm doing this.

We can all have a good laugh and relax when I tell them the truth.

April turned back to Dolores. The poor girl must be so dizzy, she thought. It's time to signal her to stop.

April waved both hands at Dolores and shouted some strange-sounding words.

Did Dolores see the signal? April gave it again.

Why doesn't she stop?

To April's surprise, Dolores spun faster—*and lifted off the floor*!

The room rang out with screams as, spinning wildly, her arms flailing, Dolores floated up off the floor. She spun in midair, three feet off the floor.

Then floated higher.

April watched Dolores's face twist in terror—*real* terror.

"Help me! Oh, help!" she shrieked. "April—stop it! April—please!"

Josh and Rick ran into the center of the room. Jumping. Reaching up. Desperately, they tried to grab Dolores and pull her down.

But the spinning girl rose higher, just out of their reach.

April pressed her hands against her cheeks and watched helplessly as Dolores shot up to the ceiling. Her head hit a wooden rafter with a deafening *thud*.

Dolores uttered a low groan. "Ohhhh. Please . . . somebody . . . make her stop!"

April gasped as she realized all eyes were on her now. Her three teammates had backed away from her. Still hugging herself, Kristen glared at her in disbelief.

"I—I'm not doing it!" April choked out.

Screams rang out again as the breakfast plates and glasses rose up from the tables. Eggs and toast and bowls of cereal, glasses of orange juice—all flew up from the tables, across the room.

The lights flashed on and off. Kids ducked under

tables as plates and glasses flew at them.

Dolores screamed as her head thudded against the rafter again. April watched her slam into the wall, then slide to the floor. She sprawled there in a heap—and didn't move.

The plates and glasses, the food and juice—it all clattered to the floor. Nothing moved now. An eerie silence fell over the room.

Kids climbed out from under the tables. Josh and Rick hurried over to Dolores and knelt beside her. She still hadn't moved.

April felt all eyes on her. She turned away from the accusing stares of her teammates.

And saw Donald Marks staring at her from the doorway. He was rubbing his stubbled jaw thoughtfully, staring at her, staring so hard. . . .

"I didn't do it," April whispered. "You've got to believe me. It was all a joke."

Kristen continued to eye her coldly. Marlin and Anthony hung back against the wall, looking frightened, as if they expected April to make them spin next.

"I couldn't have done that!" April shouted. "I don't have any powers."

She ran across the room to where Dolores was starting to stir. "Tell them!" April cried, bending beside her. "Dolores—tell them it was all a joke. We cooked it up last night. *Tell* them!"

Dolores gazed up at her blankly. "Go away," she whispered. "Please, April—don't hurt me anymore."

April could feel Donald Marks's eyes on her as she made her way with the other kids along the shore to the rock-climbing competition.

Josh led the way. He was in charge of the competition. But Marks had trailed along to watch.

Dolores, who was on Team One, was feeling better. As they walked to the sloping hills of blue rocks, she kept as far away from April as she could.

The others made their way over the sand in twos and threes. For the most part, team members stuck together. But April found herself walking alone.

Her teammates wouldn't even *look* at her. The three of them walked far up ahead, chattering nonstop in whispered tones.

April knew they were talking about her.

Everyone here thinks I'm some kind of witch now, April thought miserably. I'm an outcast. A total outcast. Most of them are *terrified* of me.

What can I do? What can I do to prove to them that I'm just a normal kid? That I didn't make

Dolores and everything go out of control?

What *did* happen to Dolores?

April had asked herself that question over and over. What strange force made Dolores twirl into the air like that? What made the food and everything in the mess hall go crazy?

A shudder of fear ran down April's back.

Too many weird things happening here, she thought. Martine and her burst eardrums . . . the ice-cold rocks . . . the pile of bird and fish bones near the rock caves . . . Dolores flying off the ground . . .

If only she could talk to her teammates about it. But now they really were afraid of her.

Lost in her unhappy thoughts, April was surprised to see that Josh had dropped back beside her. He brushed a leaf from his wavy, dark hair and turned his dark green eyes on her.

"How's it going, April?"

She sighed. "Not great."

"Keep to the right, guys," he shouted to the others up ahead. "We're going to climb near those caves up there."

He turned back to April. "That was pretty weird back there in the mess hall."

"Everyone thinks I did it," April replied, frowning. "You think so too—don't you?"

Josh shrugged. "I don't know what to think. I don't really believe in people having powers like that."

"I don't either," April said. "And I *don't* have powers. It was supposed to be a joke. Dolores and I rehearsed it last night. It was just a joke. But . . . "

They walked on in silence. The blue rocks glowed ahead of them. "There is something strange about this island," April said.

Josh kicked a stone out of the path. "You may be right," he muttered.

April grabbed his arm and forced him to stop walking. "What do you mean? Do you mean you believe me?"

He shrugged again. "Maybe." He lowered his voice to a whisper. "I've been on this island for a month, before any kids arrived. I helped build the cabins with Rick and a bunch of other guys. And—" He stopped.

April saw Marks watching them.

"And what?" she asked.

"I had a feeling there was something strange here," Josh whispered. "The guys and I were having a party on the beach one night. And . . . I could swear I heard a voice. A woman. Humming a song."

April swallowed. "Really?"

Josh nodded. "I know, I know. The island is uninhabited. We're the only ones living on it. But I swear I heard someone humming. It was probably just something echoing in the caves. But it was totally weird."

"I found a pile of bones!" April blurted out excitedly. "Yesterday. Near the caves. Fish and bird bones. Piled up in a circle, like no animal could do it. But no one would believe me."

"Uh . . . I'm really not allowed to talk to you kids about stuff like this," Josh said. "I'm staff—right? I'll get into major trouble."

"Maybe we could do some exploring," April suggested. "Check out the caves. See if we can find something."

Josh scratched his head. "Maybe. Maybe tomorrow. If I can sneak away for a few minutes. I haven't been able to get that humming voice out of my mind."

He flashed her a thumbs-up and jogged to the head of the group. "Okay, guys—we're going to start the climb here," he announced. "The finish line is that jagged rock at the top there." He pointed.

April gazed up the hill of blue rocks. This is steeper than where I climbed yesterday, she thought.

Josh blew his whistle. He told the teams to get together for a last-minute huddle.

Kristen, Anthony, and Marlin gathered at the edge of the rocks. They glared at April as she approached.

"We don't really want you on our team," Anthony said, his face turning red. "But we don't have a choice."

"Listen, guys, the first major competition is loyalty—remember?" Kristen reminded them. "So we have to forget about how we feel about April. We have to show team loyalty—or else we're going to be eliminated in the first round."

"Give me a chance," April pleaded. "I know what

you think. But it's not true. Give me a chance to prove myself. I promise. You won't be sorry."

No one replied.

Finally, Marlin muttered, "We don't really have a choice."

Anthony stared unhappily at April. "Let's just win this rock-climbing thing, okay?"

He turned and stomped away toward the starting line. The others followed him.

I have to do really well today, April thought as the climbing competition began. She watched the four kids on Team One scampering over the slippery blue rocks.

Maybe if I help my team win this competition they'll feel a little better about me, she decided.

But a few minutes later, halfway up the rocky hill, April slipped. Her shoe caught in a crevice between two jagged stones.

Pain shot up the length of her leg.

She let out a cry. But she quickly pulled herself together. And, ignoring the pain, made her way to the top of the rocks.

Her team came in second. It won its first five points.

But April could see how disappointed her team-mates were.

April walked back to camp by herself. The others hurried ahead, eager to get some beach time in. No one looked back at her.

As she walked, April had the eerie feeling she was

being watched. She turned back to the caves. And saw a flash of movement in one of the black cave openings.

Was someone there?

Was someone hiding in that cave, watching her?

That night, Donald Marks gathered everyone together in the meeting lodge. His face was somber. He didn't greet everyone at the door with jokes and smiles, as he usually did.

Instead, he strode heavily to the front of the room. He raised his hands for silence. Then he announced, "I'm afraid I have bad news. Our special guests—the celebrities we invited—will not be able to join us."

Cries and groans rang out in the room.

I don't believe this, April thought. The invitation to The Academy *promised* those people were coming.

"I'm sure we're all very disappointed," Marks continued. "But there was a problem with the ship. And several of our guests had schedule problems."

Were they really going to come? April wondered. Or was it all a lie?

She watched Marks wipe sweat off his bald head with a white handkerchief. Around her, the other kids were shaking their heads glumly and muttering to one another.

"But there is always a bright side," Marks said. "Now we will be able to spend all of our time on the Life Games competition." He grinned at them. "And believe me, the staff and I have lots of surprises planned for you."

"A big event tomorrow!" Rick called out.

"Yeah. Tomorrow is the night hike," Josh said.

"In case it hasn't been explained," Marks said, "the three teams will be out on their own. Your team must stay out all night."

"Yaay! An all-nighter!" a boy named Jared shouted. "Parrr-tee!"

Marks laughed, then continued. "You must explore as much of the island as you can. You must go all the way to the small dock on the other side. Rick and Abby will be waiting for you to check in there. Then comes the hard part—finding your way back. And remember, you cannot return to the Academy village until the sun comes up."

"How will we be judged?" Dolores asked from the back of the room.

"The team that returns first after dawn wins," Marks replied. "But keep in mind, these contests are part of the big competition—for loyalty."

April glanced around the room at her teammates. How can we ever win a loyalty competition? They all *hate* me!

After a few more announcements, Marks told them all to get a good night's sleep. "You're going to need it!"

The kids climbed up from the benches and made their way out of the meeting lodge. As April stepped out into the warm night, Josh hurried to catch up with her.

"Still want to go exploring?" he asked in a whisper. "I'll meet you by the dock tomorrow morning, right after breakfast."

"Great!" April whispered back.

"I think you're right, April. I think there *is* something—" He stopped when he saw Marks watching them. "Catch you tomorrow!"

April hurried to her cabin. She knew she needed to get to sleep. But she felt restless, tense. She kept thinking about Dolores twirling out of control toward the ceiling. She kept picturing her terrified teammates staring at her. Accusing her.

It took her hours to fall asleep.

The next morning was a hot, steamy, junglelike day. April woke up with sweat drenching her nightshirt. Her hair stuck wetly to the back of her neck.

Today is going to be a scorcher, she thought.

She yawned and stretched. Kristen and the other two girls had already left the cabin.

"Wish I could stay in bed all day," she murmured. But then she remembered Josh and their secret plans.

She dressed quickly, pulling on a white tank-top and khaki shorts. She brushed her hair, then tugged a baseball cap down over it.

April looked for Josh at breakfast but didn't see

him. She didn't feel like eating. She was too excited. But she gulped down some orange juice and a bowl of cornflakes.

Where was Josh?

"April? Hey, April?" Marlin was shouting to her from the next table. "We're going to meet to talk about the night hike."

"I—I'm sorry," April replied. "I . . . have to do something." She jumped up and ran out of the mess hall.

Just outside, she bumped into Dolores. Dolores backed up, terror in her eyes. "Stay away from me," she snapped. She turned and headed to the cabins, arms crossed tightly over her chest.

"Dolores, I keep trying to apologize," April said, chasing after her. "But you keep avoiding me. I swear—I didn't do that to you. I don't know what happened—but it wasn't my fault."

Dolores spun around furiously. "You almost killed me!" she cried. "You tricked me into playing that dumb joke. Then you almost broke my neck."

"No!" April said, grabbing Dolores's arm. "What do you think I am? Some kind of magician or witch? I can't make people fly into the air!"

"Then why did I spin off the floor? And why did all the food fly everywhere?" Dolores demanded.

"I don't know. I really don't," April told her. "But I plan to find out. Right now."

She turned to the dock, shielding her eyes from the bright morning sun with one hand. Where was

Josh? He said he would meet her there.

"Please believe me," she said to Dolores. "Please accept my apology. I—"

But Dolores had already disappeared into her cabin.

With a sigh, April began jogging toward the dock. Small, puffy white clouds reflected in the clear water. A gull soared low over the water. It dove suddenly, pouncing on a fish. And brought up its prey, silvery and slender, flopping in the gull's beak.

One of the boats was gone, she noticed. Only one remained, bobbing gently against the wooden dock.

April searched for Josh. She turned and looked up and down the beach. No sign of him.

She wiped sweat off her forehead with the back of her hand. The sun was still low in the sky. But the air was already hot and steamy.

Kicking up sand as she walked, April made her way back to the village. She was just passing the mess hall when she felt a shadow sweep over her. Donald Marks stepped into her path.

"What's up, April?" he asked, not smiling.

"Have you seen Josh?" she blurted out.

Marks's eyes narrowed. "Didn't you hear? I thought Rick announced it at breakfast."

"Announced what?" April asked. "I was a little late for breakfast this morning."

Marks nodded. "Oh. Well . . . Josh got sick last night."

"He *what*?" April cried.

"We think maybe his appendix burst," Marks said, his eyes locked on hers. "He was in a great deal of pain. We had to rush him to the main island."

Marks spoke the next words slowly, as if they had extra meaning. And his words gave April a chill.

"I don't think Josh will be coming back."

The sun had gone down, but the air was still steamy and hot. Insects chittered in the trees. A tiny sliver of a moon floated just above the swaying palm trees.

April met her teammates after dinner in front of the meeting hall. Backpacks bulged on their backs. Kristen tilted a bottle of water to her mouth.

Anthony raised the beam of light from his flashlight to April's face. "You ready?"

April nodded. She tugged her flashlight from her backpack. She gazed around the empty camp. The other two teams had gathered near the ocean.

"I have to tell you something," April whispered. "I think something happened to Josh, and I don't think it was his appendix. That was just a story Marks told us."

Anthony rolled his eyes. "Here she goes again," he muttered.

"April, what are you talking about?" Kristen asked sharply.

"Josh and I had a plan," April replied, glancing

around again to make sure Marks wasn't around to hear her. "To go exploring. Because we both thought there is something strange on this island. Maybe someone else living here."

"Maybe the island is *haunted*!" Anthony sneered. He let out an evil movie laugh.

Marlin shook his head. "Stop this crazy talk."

"I'm not making this up," April insisted. "Marks overheard Josh and me making our plan. And today Josh is gone. Just like that."

"Josh got sick last night," Marlin said. "They announced it at breakfast. Stop trying to cause trouble, April."

April saw that they weren't going to believe her. "They think the only strange thing on this island is me," she muttered to herself.

They began walking away from the camp, following the sandy path that led into the forest. Under the low trees, the pale moonlight disappeared. The only light came from the beams of their flashlights ahead of them on the forest floor.

"This path leads to the rock caves near the shore," Marlin said. He and Anthony walked side by side, bumping each other as they walked. Kristen followed them, swinging her light over the smooth tree trunks.

April walked a few yards behind Kristen. She felt alert, excited. Over the steady chirping of insects, she heard the low warble of birds in the trees.

If only she could stop thinking about Josh . . .

"I don't know if the path goes all the way to the other side of the island," Marlin said. "We'll have to follow it and see."

"Well, we can't follow the shore. It's too rocky," Kristen said. "We have to reach Rick and Abby at the little dock by going through the trees."

"Finding our way back will be the hard part," Anthony added. "We'll be completely on the other side of the island."

"No problem!" Marlin exclaimed. April watched him tug something from his pack. A long, silvery blade glinted in the light of Kristen's flashlight.

"A machete!" Anthony exclaimed.

"That's pretty scary looking, Marlin. What are you going to do with *that*?" Kristen demanded.

Marlin grinned. He made wide chopping motions with the big knife. "Kung-fu warrior!" he cried.

"Hey—watch out!" Kristen shrank back.

Marlin lowered the machete. "This will help us find our way back," he said. "I'm going to mark the path."

He stepped up to the narrow trunk of a palm tree. He pulled the machete back, then swung the blade hard into the soft wood. *Choppp*.

April stepped up beside her teammates and squinted into the light to examine the trunk. The machete blade had sliced a narrow groove about an inch deep.

Marlin led the way deeper into the forest. Every few paces he stopped and swung the machete.

Choppp. Another slice mark in the side of a tree.

"We'll follow the cuts home," Marlin said. "We'll be back at the village while the other two teams are wandering around lost, calling for their mommies." He laughed and swung the blade.

Choppp.

"Cool!" Anthony declared. "Totally cool."

The path curved toward the shore. April could hear the waves washing against the rocks. They all stopped as a lizard was caught in the circle of light from Anthony's flashlight.

The lizard froze and stared up at them, its round black eyes reflecting the light.

"Ugly little guy," Anthony said. He raised his boot. "Should I crush him?"

"No way!" Kristen cried, pulling Anthony back. "Let him go!"

"I don't think he's ugly. I think he's cute," April said.

"Takes one to know one!" Anthony replied nastily.

The lizard suddenly came to its senses and scampered into some thick ferns. The path ended at the edge of the trees. Marlin made one more chop mark, then led the way out of the forest, toward the rock caves.

April suddenly felt a chill run down her back. Josh and I were going to explore those caves this morning, she thought. Did Marks *really* drag Josh away in the middle of the night?

What is Marks afraid of?

The blue rocks—so cold, so eerily cold all the time—were creepy during the daytime. At night they glowed softly under the moonlight.

As April approached them, the shimmering light made them appear to pulse, to throb—*as if alive!*

She blinked. Stop thinking crazy thoughts, she scolded herself. She hurried across the wet, sandy ground to catch up to the others.

"Wait up," she called. And then, as she stepped up beside them, April let out a cry.

"Stop!" she uttered, her voice shrill with terror.

A shudder of fear shook her body. She grabbed Marlin's arm. "Stop! Do you hear it? Voices! Voices! From that cave!"

The others stopped. Kristen gasped. The flashlight slipped from Anthony's hand. Listening hard, he made no attempt to pick it up.

Marlin was the first to laugh.

"April, you jerk," he muttered.

April realized she was gripping his arm. She let go and backed away. "Huh?"

"Of *course* you hear voices," Marlin said, rolling his eyes. "It's the kids on the other team."

April let out a long whoosh of air. "Oh, wow. Sorry."

She gazed up at the rocks and saw Dolores. She recognized her from her long, blond hair. Dolores was climbing on a sloping rock hill with her three teammates.

April took a deep breath. Get it together, she instructed herself. Get it together—now.

I'm letting my imagination run away with me, April decided. I've got to shape up. I've got to relax and try to show my teammates that I'm not crazy.

The three teams were not supposed to explore together. So Marlin turned away from the caves and led the way back into the trees.

Kristen and Anthony were talking together, still laughing about April's voices. "Listen, guys—I said I was sorry," April said. "I'll shut up. I promise. I won't say another word the rest of the night."

"That's okay," Marlin said. "Come on, everyone. Let's try to be a real team. It's going to be a long night. Let's have some fun!"

He swung the machete—*choppp*—and made another slice mark in the smooth trunk of a tree.

"Hey, let me try that!" Anthony said. He grabbed the big knife from Marlin's hands.

"Watch out—" Marlin cried.

Anthony swung the blade into a tree. *Choppp.* "Cool!" he cried. He pulled the blade back—and swung again. This time he made an even deeper cut below the first cut.

"Hey—you're hurting the tree!" Kristen protested.

She grabbed the handle of the machete and tried to tug it away from Anthony. The two of them wrestled with it until Marlin stepped up and took it away from them.

"Just one cut in a tree," Marlin said. "It's not for fun. It's so we can get back."

"Where are we?" April asked.

The leaves overhead had grown thicker until they blocked the sky from view. The pale moonlight couldn't break through the thick tangle of trees.

It's much darker here, April realized. And quiet. The insects had suddenly stopped chirping. April listened for the wash of the ocean waves on the shore. Silence.

"We must be somewhere in the middle of the island," Marlin said. "If we just keep going straight . . . "

"But the path ends here," Kristen said. She swept her flashlight over the trees. "Which way is straight?"

"We have to keep going north," Marlin said. He pulled off his baseball cap and wiped his forehead with his hand. "Man, it's hot tonight. Wish we could go for a swim."

"Which way is the ocean?" April asked. "I—I'm all turned around."

"I brought a compass," Anthony said, pulling off his pack. "It's supposed to point toward the north, right?" He squatted down and unzipped the pack.

Kristen leaned over Anthony and held her light on the pack while he searched through it. He pulled out a water bottle and took a long drink.

"Take your time," Marlin said sarcastically. "We're only lost here in the middle of the island."

"Don't worry. The other teams are probably even *more* lost," Anthony said. "Hey—here it is."

He pulled out a round object on a leather strap. "My grandfather gave me this compass when he came back from Alaska. He was a gold prospector in the Yukon and—"

"Save the family history for later," Kristen said.

She shone her light on the compass. "Well? Which way do we go? Which way is north?"

Anthony squinted hard at the compass dial. He turned it in his hand. Then he turned it again.

Suddenly, he jumped to his feet. "Whoa! I don't believe it! This can't be happening! It can't!"

He held the compass up so the others could see. April squeezed between Marlin and Kristen to get a good look.

Inside the dial, the arrow was spinning. Spinning rapidly, round and round.

"That's impossible!" Anthony cried. "Why is it doing that?"

"Because it's broken," Marlin said, frowning.

"A compass can't break," Anthony cried. "It's magnetic. That's all. It's just a magnet. What would make it spin like that?"

April stared at the spinning arrow. It looked like one of those crazy clocks in cartoons.

"Put it away," Marlin muttered. He wiped sweat off his forehead again. "Ow!" He slapped his neck. "Did anyone bring mosquito spray?"

"What time is it?" Kristen asked.

Marlin shone his flashlight onto his wristwatch. He squinted at the watch for a long time. "You're not going to believe this," he whispered.

He shook his wrist hard and stared at the watch again. "It—it stopped," he said. "It stopped at seven-oh-two."

April raised her watch to the light—and let out a gasp. "Mine too!" she cried. "Look. It stopped at seven-oh-two."

"Weird," Kristen muttered. "First the compass, then the watches. That's *totally* weird."

"You're starting to sound like April," Anthony told her.

"Let's find the ocean," April suggested. "If we keep the ocean on our left, we'll be heading in the right direction."

"Then we have to go this way," Marlin said. He turned to the left and made his way toward the trees.

"No—wait!" Anthony zipped up his pack, flung it onto his shoulder, and ran after Marlin. "You're all turned around. We want to go *that* way!" He pointed to the right.

"I think Anthony is right," Kristen said. "Because we came through those trees over there—remember?" She pointed behind her.

April swept her flashlight beam over the ground. "Where is the path? If we could see where the path ended . . . "

"No, that's no help!" Kristen cried. "We came through those trees over there. I *know* we did."

All four of them began talking at once.

"Whoa! Hold it! Hold it!" Marlin shouted finally. He raised the machete high over his head.

April and the other two grew silent. Marlin looked so menacing with that blade glimmering in his hand, April felt a chill.

"We left a trail, right?" Marlin asked, waving the machete over his head. "We left a trail to follow."

"For when we want to go back," Kristen said. "But we don't want to go back."

"Why not go back?" Marlin replied.

"That's right," Anthony agreed. "We have all night."

Kristen squinted at Marlin. "What is your plan?"

Marlin pointed to the trees. "We find the chop marks and we follow them. Back to the blue rocks and the ocean."

"We go back?" Kristen asked.

Marlin nodded. "Not all the way to the village. We're not allowed there until dawn. Just to the rocks. That way, we'll get our direction back."

"Yes, that's good," April chimed in. "Then we can start through the forest again with the ocean on our left."

Anthony scratched his face. "Go all the way back to the rocks?"

"Why not?" Marlin replied. He pointed to the trees. "We could pick a direction—any direction—and just go. But why take a chance? Besides, it's not that far."

"It's a good plan," April said. "Let's stop arguing and do it."

Marlin slapped her on the back. "Hey—a little

team spirit! Now you're cooking, April!"

Everyone laughed, even Anthony. It made April feel a bit better.

Marlin headed to the trees. "Here's the last chop mark we made," he said. He shone his flashlight on the trunk.

The others started to follow him. But all four kids stopped when they heard a sound.

A loud *choppp*.

Nearby. To their right.

They turned toward the sound. "Who's there?" Marlin called.

Silence.

Then another *choppp*.

The sound of a blade cutting into a tree trunk. This one up ahead.

"Hey!" Anthony cried. "Is someone there? Who is it?"

Another *choppp* rang out through the trees. This one to their left, closer.

Marlin started running toward the sound. But he stopped at another sound of a blade slicing into a tree.

"Who is doing that?" he shouted.

"Who's there?" Kristen cried.

April swept her flashlight beam around in a fast circle. She saw only trees and ferns and low shrubs.

No one there. No one.

Chop chop . . . choppp.

All around them now. Close and far. Behind them. Up ahead. And to both sides. The swipe of a blade through the air. And the chopping . . . chopping . . .

Faster. Slice-slice-slice . . .

"I don't understand this!" Kristen said in a trembling voice. She pressed her hands to her ears as if trying to shut out the chopping. The steady, horrible chopping . . . "Make it stop! Make it stop!" she wailed.

"We've got to get out of here!" Marlin cried.

Chop . . . chop . . .

"Let's follow the path we made," Anthony said, his eyes wide with fear. "Here's the first chop mark."

Choppp . . . choppp . . . The cutting continued all around them.

"No. Here's the first one," Kristen said, grabbing a palm-tree trunk.

"This one has a slice," April said. "And this one. And look—" Her words caught in her throat.

All of them.

Every tree!

Every tree trunk in the forest had a slice mark.

Who was doing it? There was no one there. No one in view.

But the horrifying sound continued to pound in their ears.

Chop . . . chop . . . choppp . . .

27

The machete trembled in Marlin's hand. He raised it in front of him like a sword.

The steady chopping sounds echoed through the forest. Far into the distance.

"Who's there?" Marlin called, waving the big knife. "Who is doing that?" He turned to the others. "This is *crazy*! This isn't happening!"

April grabbed his arm. "Let's just go," she said. "Pick a direction—any direction."

But Marlin stood there frozen, listening to the click-click-click of tree trunks being sliced.

"This way!" Kristen cried. She began running through the trees. "Come on! We're bound to come out somewhere."

April tugged Marlin after her. The three kids began running after Kristen, ducking under low branches, pushing their way through tangles of vine.

"We've got to get to Rick and Abby on the other side," Anthony said breathlessly.

"We've just got to get away from here!" Kristen replied.

"Hey—listen." April stopped short. She leaned against a slender palm trunk, breathing hard. The trunk had a notch in it at about the height of her waist.

"It stopped!" Marlin said. "The chopping—it finally stopped."

They could hear the chirping insects again. And the rustle of the wind through the palm leaves.

"Let's keep going," April said. "The island is tiny. We must be near the shore."

"But what was that *about*?" Anthony cried, his voice shaking.

They made their way single file through the trees. April saw that every tree had a slice mark in it.

Her pack suddenly felt as if it weighed a thousand pounds. The back of her shirt was drenched with sweat.

Tall reeds slapped against her as she walked. She lowered her shoulder, pushing weeds and shrubs out of her way.

In the distance, she saw tiny, flickering dots of light—fireflies. Normally, she would have stopped to admire the magical scene.

But not tonight. Tonight was too strange, too frightening.

They were lost in this steamy, hot forest where the watches stopped, the compass spun out of control, and invisible blades sliced the trees.

"How long have we been walking?" Anthony groaned. He stopped in a small, sandy clearing and dropped his pack to the ground. He mopped his forehead with his T-shirt sleeve.

"At least half an hour," April replied. Her dark bangs were matted to her forehead with sweat. She swept her flashlight over the clearing. "Half an hour, and we haven't gotten anywhere."

April sat down on the ground and sighed. "The forest isn't that big. We should have reached the shore by now."

Marlin's eyes flashed. A strange grin spread over his face. "I know what this is," he said. "I know what's happening here!"

"I'll bet this is all part of the Life Games," Marlin said. "Yes! I'll bet Marks planned this whole thing. The chopped trees—that's all special effects or something."

Anthony squinted at him. "Special effects? You're kidding—right?"

"No. I'm serious," Marlin said excitedly. "Don't you see? This was supposed to happen. We were supposed to get lost. And we were supposed to be frightened. It's all planned. It's all part of the game."

Kristen gazed at Marlin thoughtfully. "Maybe you're right," she said softly. "But we're still lost—right? We still have to find our way to the little dock, then back to the village."

With a groan, April climbed to her feet. "I guess we should keep going," she said. "We'll just continue in a straight line. The shore has got to be right over there."

"The shore has to be *somewhere*," Anthony said wearily. "This *is* an island—right?"

"A very tiny island," Kristen said.

They continued walking. No one spoke. The fireflies sparkled all around, moving with them, as if following them.

April finished the water in her bottle. Sweat ran down her face. Her whole body itched. Her muscles ached.

"This isn't right," she said after at least an hour had passed. "Something is terribly wrong. You can walk the whole island and back in less than an hour."

Kristen sighed. "This forest just doesn't end. It's as if it keeps stretching and stretching in front of us."

Anthony shoved his face into Marlin's and sneered. "Still think it's special effects?"

Marlin gave Anthony a hard shove with both hands. "Back off. Give me a break, punk."

Anthony swung his backpack, trying to hit Marlin with it.

"Guys—break it up!" Kristen cried, jumping between them. "We can't start fighting now."

"Yes. What if this is part of the loyalty test?" April said.

"You shut up!" Anthony snarled, swinging toward April. "Your opinion is *so* not wanted! Are you using your evil powers on us? Is that what this is? Are our eardrums going to explode now?"

April backed away, hurt.

"Shut up! Anthony, shut up!" Kristen pleaded. "You're totally losing it. Again."

"We've got to keep it together," Marlin said. He

handed Anthony his water bottle. "Here. There's a little left."

Anthony slapped it away. "I'm sick of this. I just want to get back to the village."

"And are you sick of a hundred thousand dollars?" Marlin snapped. "Are you forgetting why we're here? Are you going to blow it for all of us?"

Anthony rolled his eyes but didn't reply. He angrily kicked Marlin's water bottle into the trees. "Let's get moving," he muttered.

They adjusted their packs and began trudging through the forest again. How much time passed? April lost track.

Finally, she saw a ribbon of pink in the sky. "I don't believe it!" she gasped. "The sun. It's almost dawn."

"We've walked all night," Kristen said, yawning wearily.

"The sun rises in the east, right?" Marlin said. He pointed. "So that's north and south."

Anthony raised a finger to his lips. "Listen!"

In the hush, April heard a familiar sound, the soft splash of waves breaking over rocks. "The ocean!" she cried. "We've finally found it!"

A few minutes later, they stepped out from the trees—and found themselves staring through the hazy dawn at the hills of blue rocks. Pink sunlight splashed over the caves and smooth stones, giving them a rosy glow.

"YAAAY!" Marlin cheered, shooting his fists into

the air. He went running to the rocks. "We'll cross the rocks and follow the beach back to the village!" he cried.

Packs bouncing on their backs, April and the others took off, following Marlin down the slippery, sloping rock hill. The red morning sun reflected in the ocean, making it shimmer with purple.

The whole world is glowing with color! April thought, so happy that the long night was nearly over.

She gasped when she heard a startled cry.

Turning back, she saw that Marlin was down on the ground in front of a dark cave opening. How had he fallen behind? she wondered.

"It's okay," he called. "I slipped, that's all. No problem!"

April watched him climb to his feet. Then she took off again, following Kristen and Anthony along the yellow sand.

A short while later, they burst breathlessly into the village. April gazed around the empty grounds until she spotted Rick and Abby. They had a supply shed open and were putting equipment away. The rest of the camp was deserted.

"Hey! We're back!" Anthony shouted.

The two staff members turned to greet them. "Quiet—you'll wake the others," Rick warned.

"They all got back a long time ago," Abby said. "Where were you guys? You didn't even make it to the little dock."

"Abby and I were worried about you," Rick said.

"We kind of got lost," Anthony replied.

"Well, at least you made it," Abby said. "You can get some sack time now. You've been up all night." She turned to Rick. "So have we. I'm beat. See you all later."

Rick locked the supply shed. Then he and Abby headed to their cabins.

April turned to Anthony and Kristen. "What a night," she sighed. "I can't wait to get some shut-eye. Hey—where's Marlin?"

"Huh? He was right behind us," Kristen said.

April gazed down to the beach. Empty. No sign of him.

She cupped her hands around her mouth and called, "Marlin? Marlin?"

A chill swept down her back. "Where *is* he?" she cried. "He's . . . gone!"

29

"He'll be here any second," Anthony said, yawning. His red hair was matted to his head. Rivers of dirt ran down the sides of his face.

"But where *is* he?" April demanded.

"Maybe he stopped to admire the sunrise over the water," Kristen said. She yawned too. "Whatever," she muttered. "I'm falling asleep standing up." She started toward the cabin. "You coming?"

April shook her head. She kept her eyes on the beach. "In a sec. I just want to make sure Marlin is okay."

Kristen and Anthony disappeared to their cabins. April tossed her pack on the ground and dropped down on it. "Where are you, Marlin?" she asked out loud.

The sun rose higher in the sky. April rested her head in her hands. I'm going to fall asleep sitting up, she thought.

She looked up to see Donald Marks walking slowly toward his office. He was wearing gray sweats, stretching his arms up over his head as he walked.

"Mr. Marks!" April called out. She climbed to her feet and hurried over to him.

"April? Why aren't you asleep?" Marks asked.

"We just got back. From the hike," she replied. "Only Marlin didn't come back."

Marks narrowed his eyes at her but didn't say anything.

"We came down over the rocks. He was right behind us," April explained. "But then . . . he was gone."

Marks shrugged his broad shoulders. "No problem," he said quietly. "He'll show up."

"But I'm worried about him," April said shrilly. "He fell at the caves. He said he was okay, but what if—"

"Go get some sleep," Marks replied. "You've been up all night, April. You must be exhausted."

"But Marlin—?"

"I'll deal with it," he said, starting his stretching exercises again. "Now go. It's not your problem, understand?"

April nodded. She picked up her pack and started wearily toward her cabin.

But when Marks was out of sight, she stopped. Why wasn't he upset about Marlin? she wondered. He didn't even seem surprised. He didn't seem to care at all.

What if Marlin is hurt? What if he's in some kind of trouble?

April tossed her pack against a tree. I'm going back to the rocks, she decided.

I can't leave Marlin back there. I'm going to find him and figure out what happened.

She knew Marks could see her from his office. But she didn't care. She took a deep breath and began jogging to the beach.

Her sneakers thudded over the wet sand. The low red sun made the ocean water glow with color. Hovering over the water, two gulls squawked and fought over a silvery fish.

The beach was deserted. No sign of Marlin.

As April drew near the blue rocks, a strong wind came up suddenly, howling and swirling. It swept sand high into the air—sheet after sheet of sand—and blew it against her as she jogged.

Coughing, blinking, April lowered her head and struggled on. But the sudden wind came in powerful gusts, sweeping the sand at her. Pushing her back . . . Pushing her.

As if trying to keep me away, she thought.

Holding her hands in front of her face, she lowered her shoulder into the wind. Slowly, painfully, she made her way forward.

The wind died as she approached the rock hills. April shook sand from her hair as she began to climb.

The rocks were slippery and wet beneath her

shoes. And so cold. She could feel the cold shimmering up from the rock surface.

Her legs ached from her long night of hiking. She felt dizzy, off balance. But she pulled herself higher. Higher . . .

The caves stood just above. April opened her mouth to shout Marlin's name.

But her breath caught in her throat—and she gasped as she saw the woman on the rocks above her.

Yes! A woman!

April could see the woman's long, brown hair falling over her black cloak. She had pale white skin.

A mist rose up over the rocks. A cold, dark mist.

The woman appeared to be floating in the mist. Rising from it, as if the mist were part of her body.

A woman! A woman!

There *is* someone else on this island! April realized.

Josh said he heard a woman humming. He was right!

And what is she doing? April wondered.

Surrounded by the heavy, dark mist, the woman was bending over something.

April climbed higher, struggling to see. There were no shadows to hide in, no trees. She just had to hope that the woman didn't look her way.

The woman bent low. April squinted hard, trying to see clearly in the bright glare of sunlight.

Someone else was up there, April realized.

She could see a figure lying on the rocks. Sprawled on his back, half covered in the swirling, dark mist.

Marlin!

Yes. April recognized Marlin.

The woman in the black cloak leaned over him. She pressed her face against Marlin's.

April's whole body trembled, partly from the icy cold of the rocks, partly from what she was seeing.

Was the woman blowing air into Marlin's mouth? Was she trying to revive him? Was it CPR?

Her legs shaking, chill after chill raced down her body, April edged closer.

Close enough to see Marlin's chest heave. And his stomach go in when the woman lowered her lips to his.

Oh, wow, April thought. Oh, wow.

She shuddered again as the horror swept over her.

The woman was *sucking out* Marlin's breath!

Marlin let out a hoarse cry of pain. The cry was muffled by the woman's lips. She lowered her head over his.

Now Marlin let out a weak cry. And another. Another. Each cry grew weaker.

He raised his arms as if to fight her off. But his arms fell limply to his sides.

Again she lowered herself to him.

Sucking out his breath . . . Sucking away his strength . . .

"NO! STOP!" The cry burst from April's throat.

The woman raised her head. Her hair flew up about her, disappearing into the mist. Her dark eyes glowed like fiery coals.

She turned—and raised her hand.

And pointed her finger at April.

April froze and couldn't move.

"What took you so long?" April asked Marlin. "We got back to the village, and you weren't there."

"I—I don't know," Marlin replied, shaking his head. "I don't remember. I—I just feel so weak, so tired. And my chest—it aches."

It was a few minutes later. They were walking side by side along the beach. The waves lapped gently at the shore. April carried her shoes in her hand. The wet sand felt good on her hot feet.

"How did you find me?" Marlin asked.

April thought hard. "I don't remember," she said finally. "Weird! I remember running from the village to find you. But after that . . . it's all a blur."

She turned and gazed back at the blue rocks. They glowed like jewels under the morning sun.

No one there.

Why did she have the feeling she had seen something back there? Why did she have the feeling that something had happened, something unpleasant?

Something lingered in her mind. Something she

knew she should remember.

Something *too frightening* to remember?

Suddenly, her head felt as if it would split in two. She rubbed her temples. "Whoa. I have a major headache," she murmured.

"Me too," Marlin said. "I guess it's because we were up all night. And all the craziness . . . "

April saw Marks waiting for them near the dock.

Uh-oh, she thought. Am I in trouble?

To her surprise, Kristen and Anthony appeared beside Marks.

As Marks jogged out to greet April and Marlin, a smile spread over his face. "Congratulations!" he boomed. He shook hands solemnly with April, then with Marlin.

"What did we do?" Marlin asked, confused.

"Your team has just won the loyalty contest," Marks announced.

All four kids let out cries of surprise.

"We won? But *how*?" Kristen asked.

Marks put a hand on April's shoulder. "Actually, April won the competition for you. She knew she wasn't supposed to go out looking for Marlin. But she did it anyway. She put her loyalty to a teammate above everything else."

Anthony's face twisted in confusion. "*April* won the competition for us?"

Marks nodded, still grinning.

"Way to go, April!" Marlin cried. He slapped her a high-five. And then there were cheers and high fives all around.

April felt happy to be the hero for once. Maybe now they will accept me and forget that other nonsense, she thought.

As they all started to walk to the cabins, Kristen turned to Marlin. "Where *were* you anyway?" she asked. "What happened?"

Marlin frowned at her. "I'm not sure," he replied. "It's all . . . kind of cloudy."

"Well, what was he doing when you found him?" Kristen asked April.

April thought hard. A feeling of panic choked her throat. Why couldn't she remember?

"I—I'm not sure," she told Kristen. "He was still on the blue rocks. Near a cave. I remember that. But . . ."

"You're just overtired," Marks told them. "You're exhausted from being up all night. And it's playing tricks with your memory."

They had reached his office. He waved them away with both hands. "Get some shut-eye. I'll see you all later. Congratulations again. We'll announce your victory at dinner tonight."

Excited by their win, the kids trotted over the sand to their cabins. "What's the next big competition?" Anthony asked.

"Honesty," Marlin answered, yawning.

"No problem," Anthony said. "We'll take that one too."

April followed Kristen into their cabin. The other

two girls were sound asleep. They didn't stir when Kristen and April entered.

April was too tired to change. She fell onto her bed with her clothes on. It took only seconds to fall into a deep, dreamless sleep.

April slept most of the day. It was late afternoon when she finally managed to climb out of bed, shower, and pull on a bathing suit.

She had a short, refreshing swim. Then joined a few other kids catching the late afternoon sun on the beach.

Where is everyone? she wondered. The village seems awfully empty today.

At dinner, she was surprised to find that one of the tables had been removed from the mess hall. April took a seat beside Kristen, then counted the kids at the table. Only eight.

"Where is Dolores?" she asked Kristen.

Kristen shrugged.

"Dolores and her whole team aren't here," April said.

April spotted Marks heading to join Rick and Abby at the staff table against the wall. She jumped up and ran to block his path.

"Mr. Marks, hi. Can I ask you something? Where are the other kids?" She pointed to the table.

Marks cleared his throat. He gazed past her. "They've been eliminated," he said, almost in a whisper.

April swallowed. "Excuse me? I don't understand. Are they somewhere else on the island? Did you send them home?"

To April's surprise, Marks's expression turned cold. And he fixed her with an icy stare. His reply was spoken through gritted teeth:

"I told you. They've been *eliminated*."

All part of the games, April thought. Being eliminated is part of the competition.

But why does it sound so creepy when Marks says it?

She decided not to dwell on it. She and her teammates had to rest up for another competition the next afternoon.

"This is fun!" Kristen cried. She paddled her kayak beside April's. "I've never done this before. These little boats are so cute!"

The waves banged the two kayaks together. "Careful!" April shouted. "The waves are pretty choppy this morning. I'm afraid of tipping."

Kristen laughed as their kayaks bumped again. Then she paddled out toward their teammates. "Hurry, April. Line up. The race is about to start."

"Ten more points! Ten more points!" Marlin was chanting. He waved for the two girls to hurry.

April had watched Rick and Abby pull nine or ten

133

yellow kayaks from the supply cabin that morning. She didn't know how well she would do in a race. But she was eager to take one out and try it.

This is what a fish must feel like, she thought. I'm so low in the water, and I can glide so easily.

A sharp wind tossed the green waves, making the kayaks rock. High clouds turned the sky pale, the color of skim milk.

April glanced to shore and saw Marks watching from the dock. She turned away from him and began paddling to the others.

"Whoa!" Jared, a boy on the other team, slid his kayak in front of her. The front of April's kayak thudded into Jared's side.

"How's it going, April?" Jared called, bobbing in front of her.

"Fine. Till you got in my way," April replied.

"What's up?" Clark, a boy on Jared's team, bumped up behind April. "Are you trying to ram Jared's kayak?" he asked April.

"No way!" April said. "He bumped me!"

"I saw you—cheater!" Jared teased. "Bumping isn't allowed—is it?" He dug his paddle furiously into the water—sent his kayak sailing forward—and bumped April's kayak hard.

Both boys laughed.

"See if you're laughing at the end of the race!" April declared. She slapped her paddle into the water and sent a spray of water into Jared's face. Then, swinging her kayak around, she paddled away from them.

Bobbing in place in their kayaks, Rick and Abby waited for the eight racers to line up. "The race starts and ends here," Rick announced. "All the way around the island, guys. The first team to make the complete circle wins the race."

April's heart began to pound. She felt her muscles tense.

I've never been in a kayak in my life, she thought. Can I really make it all the way around the island?

The whistle blew. The eight racers furiously pounded the water with their paddles. The kayaks slid easily, low in the rocking waves.

We're going against the waves now, April realized. It will be easier and faster coming back, when we're paddling with the current.

Marlin pulled out from the line of yellow boats to take an early lead. April saw Clark gliding close behind Marlin. The two kayaks were soon far ahead of the pack. A girl named Ronni was a distant third.

April paddled steadily, trying to get the right rhythm. The waves rolled high over the front of the kayak, sending a cold spray over her.

I'm falling behind, she thought.

She turned and saw a kayak behind her, moving fast to catch up. As it drew nearer, she recognized Jared. Paddling hard, his face was red, his features set in a determined scowl.

April turned away and concentrated on keeping her fast, steady rhythm. The kayak began to glide a little more smoothly.

"I'm not going to be last!" Jared shouted. "No way!"

She ignored him and kept to her rhythm. The palm trees on the shore slid past, giving way to the outcropping of blue rocks.

"No way I'm last!" Jared cried behind her. "No way!"

And then he wasn't behind her. His kayak was *beside* her, high in the water, sailing fast. Again April saw his red face knotted in anger.

"STOP!" she shouted. "You're going to hit me!"

They both screamed as Jared's kayak slammed hard into April's side, a vicious hit.

April's scream was cut off by cold water—as her craft overturned and her head plunged below the surface.

Choking, flailing with the paddle, she hung upside down. The green water rushed around her.

And then she felt herself falling.

Falling from the kayak. Still gripping the paddle, she plunged down . . . down.

She could see so clearly. She could see a crusty wall of red coral rising up from the ocean floor. And yellow sunfish, dozens of them, hovering like butterflies on the coral.

Raising her head, she saw the kayak floating high above her on the surface.

Her chest felt about to burst. She let go of the paddle, raised her arms above her head, and felt the rubber life jacket begin to lift her.

Up, up. She burst through the surface of the

136

water, gasping for air, choking, taking breath after breath.

Bobbing on the waves, she saw Jared's kayak far in the distance now, rounding a curve of the island, vanishing out of sight.

That cheater! I *am* going to be last, she thought bitterly.

She turned to the shore—

—and opened her mouth in a startled scream.

A woman. Cloaked in black. A woman with pale skin and long, brown hair flying wildly around her head.

The woman stared coldly at April, then raised a hand. Pointed a long finger at her. Cried out words in a strange language.

April felt a tug at her feet. Something began to pull her. Pull her down. A powerful force.

She thrashed her arms. Tried to kick.

But she was sinking below the surface.

The last thing April saw before the water closed over her was the red-lipped grin on the woman's face.

The water bubbled furiously around her. Her ears rang with the roar of the water.

She squirmed and struggled. Shot her arms up. Tried to kick free.

But the invisible force pulled her down and held her. And through the roar of the water and the thudding of her own heart, April heard laughter. The high, shrill laughter of the woman on the rocks.

What is happening to me? What is holding me down? Why can't I float to the top? Is that woman doing this?

Desperate questions flashed through April's mind as she kicked and strained. And felt the pain spread over her chest.

I've got to breathe. . . . Got to breathe . . .

The water suddenly appeared darker. She could no longer feel the cold. No longer see the surface . . .

Or feel the pain of her lungs about to burst . . .

I'm fading, she realized. Everything is fading away.

The water darkened more. Too dark to see.

I've got to breathe. Got to open my mouth now.

I'm fading. . . . She stopped squirming, stopped struggling. April's body went limp.

Total darkness fell over her.

And then . . .

She felt a tug.

Were those hands on her shoulders? Strong hands pulling her up?

April opened her eyes, but she still couldn't see.

The water bubbled and churned.

Her arms hung limply at her sides. Her legs were useless weights.

But something was pulling her up from the bottom.

She reached the surface, choking and sputtering. Water spewed from her mouth as she struggled to take in air.

Her whole body shuddered. Her chest ached. She spewed up more water.

Where am I?

Feeling dazed, she raised her eyes—and saw Kristen. And realized she was sprawled over the front of Kristen's kayak.

"I came back," Kristen said, holding on to April's arm. "I saw you didn't make the turn, so I came back."

April gazed at the rocks on the shore. No one there.

Had someone been standing there? She couldn't remember.

Why did she have the strange feeling that someone had been there watching her?

She turned back to Kristen. "You—you saved me," April choked out, her throat raw, her heart still pounding.

"No, I didn't," Kristen replied, studying April.

"Didn't you pull me out?" April asked.

Kristen shook her head. "No. I saw you, April. How did you do it? I saw you pull yourself up. I saw you lift yourself right out of the water."

April gasped. "Huh?" Her head spun. "Kristen— what do you *mean*?"

Kristen's eyes narrowed on April. "I never touched you. But I saw you fly up over the water. You have strange powers—don't you!" she said.

"N-no," April stammered. "I—I'm so confused, Kristen. I really don't understand."

"Go ahead. Admit it, April. I saw you. I saw what you did. You do have powers—don't you!"

A short while later, April saw Marlin and Anthony running to greet them as they made their way back to the village.

"What happened?" Anthony cried angrily. "Where were you two? We lost the race because of you."

"April had an accident," Kristen replied. "We'll tell you about it later. First we have to get her dried off."

The two boys glared suspiciously at April.

"An accident?" Anthony asked. "How could you have an accident? We really needed to win that race."

Marlin put a hand on Anthony's shoulder. "Easy, man. Accidents happen. You can see she's drenched. Give her a break."

April turned to see Marks approaching. "I was about to send the coast guard out for you two," he said. "What happened?"

"Jared rammed my kayak," April said, her voice still hoarse and clogged. "He tipped me over, and I

141

fell out. Kristen came back to save me."

Marks studied them both. His face settled into a hard frown. "The other team told me they won fair and square," he said finally. "But Jared cheated, didn't he?"

Marks turned to Abby, who was piling the kayaks back into the equipment shed. "Get the other team," he called. "Tell them to get out here—right away."

Jared, Clark, and their two teammates soon joined them. They were looking very pleased with themselves, having won the kayak race. Jared kept grinning at April, as if he had won a tremendous victory.

But Marks's words quickly made their smiles fade. "You won the kayak race," he told them. "But did you forget that the second Life Games competition is for honesty?"

"Whoa. Hold on—" Jared started to say.

But Marks cut him off with a sharp look. "The honesty competition is won by Team Three—April, Kristen, Marlin, and Anthony," he announced, staring hard at Jared. "Your team is *eliminated*."

April felt a shiver. That word again. *Eliminated*.

Her teammates began cheering, shouting, slapping high fives and hugging each other—a wild celebration.

We made it to the final game, April realized. She gazed at her happy teammates. If we win this game, we'll split a hundred thousand dollars.

Can we do it?

. . .

Late that night, April was awakened from a sound sleep by noises. She sat up on her cot, rubbing her eyes, listening.

Voices outside. A loud *bump*.

From the dock?

She had been sleeping in shorts and a sleeveless T-shirt. She pulled on sneakers and ran outside without lacing them.

It was a hot, damp night. Not a breeze. The trees didn't move.

Turning to the dock, she saw two beams of light. From the boats.

Was someone taking the boats out at this time of night?

"April, what's up?" Kristen crept up behind her.

"I'm not sure," April replied.

She saw Anthony and Marlin step out from their cabin across the path. "Hey—someone's in the boats!" Marlin exclaimed.

The four of them began jogging toward the dock.

As they came closer, April saw Marks and Rick. Rick jumped onto the boat on the left. Marks hopped on after him.

"Where are they going?" Kristen asked in a shrill whisper.

"Hey—the other kids are on the second boat," Marlin said, pointing.

The twin beams of light swept over the village, then across the trees. The boat motors roared as the boats pulled away from the dock.

"Hey, wait!" Anthony cried. "I don't believe this!"

"They're leaving! They're all leaving!" April shouted.

"Why are they leaving us here?"

As she passed Marks's office, she glanced in through the window. Empty. He had taken all his stuff.

The doors of the meeting lodge and the mess hall had been left wide open. Empty inside.

They're taking everything with them! she realized.

The dark water churned. The engine roar grew fainter as the boats sped off into the darkness.

April and her friends ran to the dock. "Wait! Wait!" They began waving frantically and shouting.

"Come back! Hey—where are you going?"

A few seconds later, the boats had melted into the night blackness.

Silence now, except for the gentle wash of the waves against the dock pilings.

"They can't do this!" Marlin cried, shaking his head. "They took everything and left us here. How are we supposed to survive?"

"I don't understand," Kristen said in a tiny voice. "The letter Marks wrote to us didn't say anything about being *stranded* on this island. No adults. Nobody!"

"They're not coming back," Anthony muttered. "They took everything. They left the island bare!"

He kicked the sand angrily. "We're stranded here. With no food. And no way to get home."

"Is Marks crazy?" Kristen asked. "This can't be part of the competition. Why did he do it?"

No one had an answer. They stared out at the water for a long time. Then they turned and started trudging slowly back to their cabins.

And as April made her way, gazing at the empty, abandoned village, she heard something . . . a voice on the wind. . . .

She stopped and tilted her head to listen.

What was it?

A woman humming?

TO BE CONTINUED . . .

What will you find next in

the NIGHTMARE rOOm?

THE NIGHTMARE ROOM THRILLOGY
FROM THE MASTER OF HORROR, R.L. STINE

ISBN 0-06-441041-2

**THE SECOND OF A THREE-PART SPECIAL...
THE NIGHTMARE ROOM THRILLOGY #2:**
What Scares You the Most?

April, Anthony, and the other Academy members are haunted by their experiences on the island. They soon discover that they are still bound by the evil they encountered there. And the only way they can rid themselves of it is to return.

THE NIGHTMARE ROOM THRILLOGY #3: NO SURVIVORS
Coming in August!

**£3.99 PAPERBACK.
AVAILABLE WHEREVER
BOOKS ARE SOLD.**

www.thenightmareroom.com
REGISTER NOW!